A GHETTO
SOLDIER

A GHETTO SOLDIER

I Came to Bring the Rain

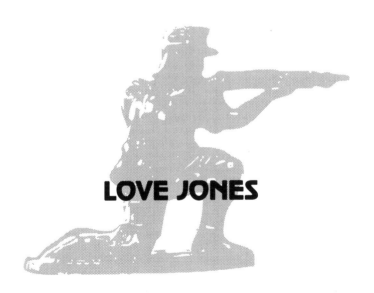

LOVE JONES

iUniverse, Inc.
Bloomington

A GHETTO SOLDIER
I CAME TO BRING THE RAIN

This is a work of fiction. All of the characters, names, incidents, organizations, and dialogue in this novel are either the products of the author's imagination or are used fictitiously.

iUniverse books may be ordered through booksellers or by contacting:

iUniverse
1663 Liberty Drive
Bloomington, IN 47403
www.iuniverse.com
1-800-Authors (1-800-288-4677)

ISBN: 978-1-4620-3988-3 (pbk)
ISBN: 978-1-4620-3990-6 (clth)
ISBN: 978-1-4620-3989-0 (ebk)

Printed in the United States of America

iUniverse rev. date: 07/09/2011

DEDICATION

For my kids:

Tameeka, Shaunta', Tondalya, Nephatiara, Love Jones, La'nostalgia, Dorothy, William, Lashaneen, Okyonna, and Jahnnae.
Excuse is the Mother who gave birth to a child name Failure. So wherever you find one . . . you'll find the other!

. . . Big Love Jones

PROLOGUE

Wearing a black valor, jogging suit, Junior Washington—better known to those who watched the news as the Ghetto Soldier, and a vigilante to the many different police task forces after him—sat behind the wheel of his car looking through a pair of night-vision binoculars. Although there weren't many people walking the streets at this time, the early morning darkness and the car's tinted windows concealed his identity from any possible probing eyes. The nearly non-existent sound coming from the car's idle engine told that the car was brand new. Had it not been for the slight smoke coming from the car's exhaust pipe the fact that it was on would have gone undetected.

As he stared off into the distance, subconsciously, his fingers stroked the trigger guard of the gun curled in the lap of his hand. Though it would not be the weapon used to finalize his mission this morning, it was a means to an end, and would therefore serve its purpose.

Years ago, the tall brown skinned man had earnestly learned the art of patience. Now he was use to this shit—the waiting. It no longer wore on his nerves as it once had. It was almost second nature to him now. He now appreciated the quiet solitude that came over him just before he went out on a mission. He knew that this mission, like all the others would only bring him that much closer to accomplishing his goal; to get even with all of those responsible—for the atrocities that had been committed against his wife and daughter while he was in prison, no matter how distant or remotely connected the people were.

This work he was going to put in this morning, and it coming to fruition would be like the flip of a coin. It depended on what side the coin landed. If the two men he sought came out of the club down the block with Summer-Bunnies on their arms, he would have to abort the mission until a later time. But if they were alone . . . .

As if through post-hypnotic suggestive thinking, seconds later the people he sought appeared on the lens of his binoculars exiting through the club's doors a short distance away. He studied the lines on their intoxicated faces. They were both smiling as they walked toward their car, but they were alone. Knowing it was time to rock and roll, The Ghetto Soldier, aka Junior Washington made his move. Slipping from the shield of his car, using the shadows of the early morning darkness he closed the distance between him and the men climbing into the front seat of their car. The Ghetto Soldier's first thought was to use the ploy of distraction by asking them for a light until he noticed the car's back door was unlocked. Without prelude, quickly, he slid into the backseat of the black BMW and announced himself,

"Good morning gentlemen."

Startled, the men spun quickly in their seats facing the back.

"Ah, ah, ah, I wouldn't do that if I were you," he said noticing the men reaching for their waist. "It gets me nervous—so if either of you draw it better be Rembrandt. But since neither of you look the type to possess such talent," he barked while brandishing the ugly gun in his hand that their eyes stayed glued to, "You'd better put up your hands where my eyes can see them or else its liable to get real ugly up in here." Sensing all the sincerity in the man's demeanor both men did as they were told while asking, "Who you dude? What's your beef?"

"Yeah, what you want with us?" Neither man took notice of the nylon, noose ropes the Ghetto Soldier had pulled from his pocket.

"Who am I? Oh, I'm just the man whose gonna tie you up right now so I can frisk you for heat," Junior said as he slipped the noose around the driver's neck, tying it tightly to the expose bars on the headrest.

"And then I want some answers to my questions," he concluded, making sure the rope on the hands of the man in the passenger seat were secured tightly as well. Having frisked both men thoroughly from the back seat, he stuck the gun in his hand into the deep pocket of his jacket. When his hand reappeared it was holding an ice-pick.

"Hold-up, wait a minute. I know you . . ." the man in the passenger seat said as if suddenly remembering Junior's face, though not realizing that this admission had just sealed his own fate.

"You be down at the shock bar, yeah . . . . I remember you. But what you want with us? We ain't got no beef?"

"I see you have a good memory," the Ghetto Soldier said, sticking the ice-pick low behind the man's earlobe. "Now let's see just how good your memory really is."

Close to twenty minutes had elapsed. Having reached a dead-end with the men in the front seat, the Ghetto Soldier emerged from the back seat of their car satisfied with all the information he had received. He knew the two men would not be able to provide him or anyone else with anymore information because the dead had never been known to talk.

Getting back into his vehicle whose engine was still running idle, he pulled out from the curb. A Ghetto Soldier . . . .

CHAPTER 1

Junior Washington, using a Dark Visor helmet to conceal his identity, gunned an all black motorcycle down Nostrand Ave in the Flatbush section of Brooklyn. Although the sights he saw were mostly blurs they were familiar enough for him to know he was getting very close to home. With only a few blocks to go he began to decelerate from fifth gear. His left hand squeezed the clutch as his left foot downshift the gear to fourth. He released the clutch again, only for an instant, and repeated this process of downshifting until he was in first gear. The Ducati 916 cruised slowly now. When it got to Lenox Street he turned into the block. The Ducati came to a complete halt in front of a Co-op apartment complex in the middle of the block.

Junior Washington pulled his motorcycle up between two parked cars before dismounting. Although the streets were practically deserted at this late hour, removing his helmet, he looked up and down both ends of the street before proceeding toward his building. Though it was faint, light traces of the scent of weed met him before he reached the security booth of his building.

Seeing him first, the Jamaican security guard chimed in a thick accent, "Big up Mr. Washington!" The Jamaican, who himself was a womanizer, had often heard the women tenants in the building refer to this tenant as a good looking giant of a man.

"Hey, what's up Sharky—what's happening?"

"Every 'tings cool mon, yes!" The Jamaican said, buzzing him through the wrought iron gates which fortified the complex. The smell of weed was in the air and he thought it senseless for the security guard to be spraying air freshener outside to cover the smell.

As Junior Washington entered one of the awaiting elevators in the lobby he smelled the aroma of weed again, this time coming from a pompous tenant's apartment who lived in the building. Had the smell been coming from his apartment he knew it would had been reported to the management's office. Though he no longer smoked weed, what he remembered about it, aside from all its negative side effects, was that it made one suffer from paranoia. To him, paranoia meant to be aware, and to be aware was to be alive. And if that's what it took for the security guard to be on point, then he was all for it. A minute later, the elevator doors opened on the fifth floor and he walked noiselessly down the carpeted corridor and entered his apartment.

Inside the house Junior Washington dropped his keys on top of the desk in the vestibule as he continued through the apartment carrying a black backpack. In the bathroom, he dropped the bag to the floor and stripped off his black sweat suit. Reached into the cabinet below the sink below the mirror and removed a miniature black hefty bag. Putting the sweat suit in the bag he pulled its yellow plastic strings tight and left the bag on the floor.

He stepped out of his under wears and underneath the water of the shower. Using the bottle of Peroxide he began to bathe the wound on his shoulder while the water beat down on him. When he had gotten shot it had all happened so fast he thought the only reason he didn't feel any real pain was because he was in shock. Now he saw it was only a graze, a flesh wound. But told himself the graze could very well had been a direct hit in other areas of his body, and chided himself for having not wore his vest. That was only because previous observation of his target told him that the mark never carried a gat. He told himself he would never do it again as the reenactments of this morning's events ran across his mind. And then chided himself again for having slept on the target's woman, although the mark did not carry a gun . . . His woman did.

He had used lock picks to gain entry into the apartment and had found the target and his woman in the bedroom. He made the target get up slowly, walked him away from the dresser and out in the open to prevent him from trying anything. He had turned his back on the woman lying naked in bed when out of the corner of his eye he seen movement giving him cause to face her, but by this time she had grabbed a gat from beneath the pillow and shot him. While getting out of the line of this fire the mark had dove for cover on the floor. He saw then, as if through a magnifying glass, the woman's finger tightening around the trigger for the second time. Stepping to the side just in time, he heard a loud roar again and this time he knew he had been hit. Instinctively, his gun barked once, and though he didn't kill her, the big hole in her shoulder assured him she would be out of commission. He then made his way to the target who at this time had peed on himself. He made him get up and open the safe in the closest. Taking no chances on there being a gat inside, which there was, he made the target lay face down on the floor while he removed the gat and stacks of money which he then placed in his bag. He then made the target take the two kilos of cocaine to the bathroom and flush them down the toilet. After pulling the teeth of the target which provided him with the name of a man named Dog, he hit the target hard, five centimeters behind the left ear and laid him in the bathtub. He was about to use their telephone to call the ambulance for the woman until the faint sounds of sirens told him that one of the neighbor's had already beaten him to it, probably when they had first heard the report of gun fire. Since it was a first floor apartment instead of going back out the front door he pulled his face mask back down and climbed out of the backyard window. Creeping through the backyards he came out on the next block where his Ducati was parked.

Junior Washington surmised that the sounds from the running water might possibly wake up his wife Karla since she was a light sleeper. He doubted though that it would wake up his daughter Kim, she was a sound sleeper and could probably sleep through a thunder storm. He no longer worried about his wife questioning the hours he kept as she had done long ago and had blatantly been told to mind her business. When she persisted, he turned on her with a coldness she'd never seen before because as she learned it was reserved for others. Yet it had frightened her to the point that she realized there were many sides to him and she did not wish to see that one anymore. He knew, however, that she was aware there was something odd about the hours he kept and that it had something to do with his endless pursuit of those who had offended her and his daughter years ago as well as the seemingly endless amount of money he kept them in every since she and his daughter had been released from the hospital. Their daughter Kim was no longer in public school but private school. And his baby brother Daryle no longer used drugs or sold them.

Junior Washington popped penicillin, applied antibiotic ointment to his wound as he stood in front of the mirror and taped some gauze to his shoulder. Wrapping a towel around him, he picked up both bags; he would dispose one of them in the morning. From the threshold of his bedroom, light from the moon shined through the window allowing him to see the contour of his wife's body. She was wearing one of his Tee-shirts, it fitted her big, yet the way it was hiked up against her body revealed that she wore nothing else. Her big brown, voluptuous thighs shown in smooth contrast against the white satin bedspread. The Tee-shirt clung to her in such a way making her dime-size nipples protrude against its fabric. Aroused by this vision, he backed out of the room. Dropping the bags in the hallway closet, he checked in on his daughter, who was in her room asleep before returning to his room. He knew the air conditioner had been turned off because its humming sound, though low, kept Karla awake.

Ever since her ordeal he noticed that she did not want even the slightest sound made to go undetected by her, or so he thought. In truth, she believed that whatever her husband was doing wasn't good and that it would one day come back to haunt him—them, and when that time came she wanted to be ready. It was part of the reason she had taken nin-jit-su lessons and put in as much time as she could at the shooting range. Even Daryle, she realized, who use to talk to her about any and everything had suddenly clamed up when she tried to pump him for information regarding his older brother's activities.

Karla stirred in bed as Junior climbed in beside her. Her hand reached over drawing traces along the form of his body, it was only then that he realized she had been awake all along.

CHAPTER 2

It was Friday night, 8:23 P.M., and it was sweltering hot. Unique lay asleep on a king-size waterbed snoring loudly, which competed with the low humming sounds coming from the air conditioner. Both the t.v. and radio were off. Aside from the humming and Unique's snoring there was complete silence. Trisha, lying next to Unique, had drunk and smoked just as much weed as he had, but she lay wide awoke, partly because of his loud snoring, but also because it was Friday night and it was still so early.

Lying on her back, her eyes stared up at the ceiling as if in a trance while the thoughts in her mind played tag, hitting one after the other. She thought about how young she still was, how she looked, the people she knew, her family, and friends,—all the men she knew and the ones she'd just recently met and wondered if she was cheating herself out of something. She thought about Unique laying next to her; their arguments, the fun, their fights, his love making, and the way he made sense most of the time when they talked. She thought back to the time when he use to pamper her and take her out everywhere on the weekends—every weekend. That time seemed so long ago now. She thought about his obsession with other women which at one time made her have a low self esteem because she thought she wasn't good enough, that is, until she realized it had nothing to do with her, that he was just a womanizer. She thought about how, for so long now, all he ever did was promise to take her out, only every time that time came, at the last minute he would cancel their date with the excuse that something else of greater importance came up. She was getting tired of this shit—his shit. Trisha sighed, turned on her side to face him, and took in his features while he slept. His burnt, black-pot complexion, narrow face, and even longer-than-a girl eyelashes. Without thinking she ran her fingers ever so gentle across the circle of waves in his hair. 'Damn, I love this nigga'; she thought inwardly, 'with his skinny sexy ass, I just can't believe t—'. her thoughts were interrupted by the sharp ringing of the telephone on the night table beside Unique. She was just about to reach over for it when Unique stirred and opened his eyes, looking into Trisha's face. He reached over and picked up the phone, "Peace! Uiee speaking."

Uiee, was short for Unique.

There was no answer.

"Hello . . . Hello . . . ," Still no answer. His eyes never left Trisha's face. He slammed down the phone, "It's probably one of them faggot ass nigga's you be fucking with!" Just then Trisha wondered why she loved him, "You know Unique, you can say some of the dumbest shit sometimes. I think the only time I can truly say I love you is when you're asleep."

"So what you're saying?" He said feeling she was trying to imply she could only love him if he was dead. "The closest we can come to death is when we sleep; therefore, a sleeping person is a dead person. Only the deaf, dumb, and blind sleep—I rest. And don't nothing come to a sleeper but a dream. You can think I'm dead if you want to but my physical form will be around a long time before I return back to the essence so you c—" Unique's mouthy lecture was cut short by the ringing of the phone again. Quickly picking up the receiver again he thrust it to Trisha who stared at him with daggers in her eyes. She hesitated in taking the phone but only for a second, "Hello."

"Yo bitch, put Unique back on the phone," a threatening voice hissed.

Frowning, Trisha looked at the phone in her hand and then returned it to her ear, "Who the fuck is this?"

"Bitch, just put the motherfucker on," came the reply. Seeing the perplexed look on his lady's face Unique snatched the phone out of her hand, "This is Uiee speaking—who's this?" He sat up then climbed out of bed.

"Yeah mother," the voice said, "I know what you punk motherfuckers did last night."

"What?" Unique barked, "Who the fuck is this?"

"Don't worry about who the fuck I am nigga, just recognize that I know you and you ain't safe no more punk!" This scene made Unique think of an interlude from a Biggie Smalls record. And told himself that first thing in the morning he was getting his number changed. And then suddenly he felt stupid when another thought occurred to him and he said, "Yo, Inf'", which was short for Infinite. "Stop playing yourself nigga—the smell of punk pussy bitch on your breath is coming through the phone."

"Ha, ha, ha," Infinite laughed, "I had you nigga, don't lie, don't lie, word is bond—I had you." Unique chuckled, "Yeah, you had me going for a minute nigga—so what's the deal?"

Trisha heard her man say the name Infinite and knew it was one of his running partners. "Tell that motherfucker don't be fucking playing with me like that," she said from her side of the bed.

"Chill, it's only Inf."

"So. I don't give a fuck who it is, he don't be calling me outta my name," Trisha gabbed fiercely.

Through the phone Infinite could hear her reading him the riot act.

"Yo, tell Trisha I'm sorry man I was only kidding when I called her a bitch, but I knew it was the only way to catch ya'll out there."

"Yo, fuck her, "Unique said thinking of what she had just said to him before the phone rang for the second time.

"No! Fuck you Uiee," Trisha barked stomping out of the bedroom and into the bathroom.

"Listen." Infinite breathed, "We gotta get together and finish that business we started last night," he said referring to them cracking down on the very loose way they had been handling their business.

"No doubt, no doubt, just let me refine my physical form and I'll see you in a little while."

"Aw' ight God. Peace!" said Infinite.

"Peace." As an afterthought, Unique said, "Oh, and Yo God, how you see today's mathematics'?"

"Yo Gee; I see today's mathematics as knowledge—wisdom, all being born to understanding."

"That's peace God," Unique said, "I see today's mathematics as knowledge—wisdom, all being born to understanding—all being born to equality."

"That's peace God, you want me to add on now?" asked Infinite.

"Now cipher God, we're gonna build though, I'ma go take this shower Yo." Hanging up, Unique went into the bathroom. Trisha was in the shower with the water running full blast causing the room to resemble a sauna. The porcelain sink, the tiles on the floor, the plastic toilet seat, the glass door surrounding the tub, as well as the mirror was steamed with vapor. Using his finger Unique wrote the word "Bitches" on the mirror and then watched the graffiti disappear into steam. Dropping his briefs he stepped into the shower and looked at Trisha. She stood five feet five even, with fair skin. People referred to her as a redbone. Her hair was long and black and she had hazel brown eyes that, at times, he knew could be piercing. Trisha had a nearly non existing waist and what he referred to as a Ponderosa ass, due to the way it just sat out there by itself away from the rest of her body. Her firm round ass caused lots of people out in public to stare at it, pretty much the same way he was staring at it now. In the eyes of many as well as himself, she was model material, despite the fact that her stature was short. Squeezing liquid soap from a bottle on to the sponge in his hand, Unique began rubbing the sponge across her back in a circular motion. Slowly his hand began to gyrate down towards her cottony soft asscheeks so soft his fingers sink in to the skin. The fact that she hadn't turned around to face him told him she was still tight with him because of what he had said. After a while, giving in, she said, "You know Unique, you talk all this good shit, and all these positive things about the black man being God with all this knowledge and shit, yet you turn right around and treat the black woman, your black woman with such disrespect. You're a hypocrite cause you talk the talk but you don't walk the walk."

"Listen, I'm striving for perfection. Rome wasn't built in a day, and there isn't a man on the face of the planet earth without fault, and although I might sometime say some foul shit outta my mouth, you know I love you like cake and will always do right by you."

"Yeah, true," Trisha began to soften, "But you know right from wrong, and you don't need an example but suppose to be the example," she concluded weakly, as the thoughts of how he made a living ate at the back of her mind. In fact, she had played a great part in his success. And they were the youngest couple she knew of who owned their own house out in Jamaica Heights. She had watched him take them from nothing to something, but at times regretted having told him that he had to be ruthless. Out of the fear that one day something bad would happen to him, she refused to have a baby with him because she didn't want her kid to be without a father. She knew that if he ever found out she was using 'The Day After' pill he would kill her. Trisha continued, "And y—"

"You're right," he said cutting her off.

"Say what?"

"I said you're absolutely right my Queen, and that's why I'm so lucky to have you. Whenever I slip, you're always right there to catch me. And I know I gotta work on getting this street shit outta me and stop being a product of my environment."

"Yeah," she laughed, "And you need to start by stop polluting the atmosphere with all that foulness that be coming outta your mouth, God." I Pretending not to she continued, "I love you too Uiee, but sometimes I wonder about us. You know like, where I'm headed? And I came to realize that I'm headed wherever you take me, I just fear sometime that you don't know where you're going," taking the sponge from him she began to wash his body.

"I know where I'm headed Trisha, I know where I been, I know where I'm at right now, but most importantly is the fact that I know where I'm going and what it's going to take to get me there. So if you're trying to say you wonna bounce on me to be with someone else, don't beat around the bush just pop the clutch and keep it moving yo. I got enough problems out there on them streets to have to come home to more problems."

"You don't have to worry about me Uiee, I just want you to love me and love yourself for Christ sake!"

"Watch it!" Unique barked due to her choice of words. "Yo, check it Trish, I got to go meet up with Inf' and handle some business, but if you need me for whatever, beep me alright?"

"You see, that's also what I mean, that's what you got them for—they suppose to take care of that stuff." When she seen that her words were no longer getting through because he froze her out just that fast she said, "Yeah, alright," and turned her back on him again. He turned her back around, "Listen, I'm getting myself together Boo, just keep believing in me, okay?"

"I do believe in you and I love you, just be careful okay? I think your man Inf' is two cans short of a six pack." He knew where she was coming from, "Yeah well, you need niggas—I mean brothers around you like that cause they keep it real. Now give me some love." Trisha leaned over and kissed him and once again felt that feeling she had felt earlier about him while he was sleeping, and knew in her heart that there was no way she would ever leave Unique, "I love you Uiee," she whispered in his ear.

"Yeah, I know," Unique smiled and got out of the tub. Spurn, she tried to throw water on him when it dawned on her they would not be having sex in the shower.

Ten minutes later Unique was dressed in his old neighborhood street gear; a two piece denim polo outfit and black Jordan sneakers. He and Trisha had separate clothes closets and dressers. He pocketed his car keys while stepping into the closet pulling from the top shelf a nineteen shot Glock and three fully loaded clips. Sticking the gun underneath his vest in the center of his back, he thought about how his woman was right when she said someone else should be taking care of things. He was the brains and therefore should not have to be out there on the front line. But he also knew that if he wanted something done right he had to do it himself. And he wanted to send a message tonight and in order for it to be effective; it would require his personal touch. He reached into a sneaker box on the shelf that was filled with hundred dollar bills, and counted out fifty of them, telling himself, as he had the night before that he would put the box back into the safe later. Clipping his beeper onto his waistband, he dropped his cellular phone into one of the many pockets on his pants and then stepped out into the deep darkness of the night.

It was almost midnight, and the club in Flatbush Brooklyn, called the Ark—was jumping. It was filled beyond capacity with wall to wall people. The lighting was dark, making it difficult to see, and deliberately designed that way, giving the club's patrons the privacy and seclusion they desired. Candles, in little fishnet glasses, hosted each small round table that was occupied by at least two couples.

The musical voice of Aaron Hall, from the group formerly known as "Guy", blasted from six giant speakers strategically placed around the dance hall, giving it a surround sound. The smell of weed, mixed with cocaine, mingling with the scent of angel dust permeating the air, gave even those who didn't indulge a free euphoric high. Clanking sounds of ice cubes hitting against glass sporadically rose above chatter of conversation buzzing around the spacious room. Heineken and Guinness Stout beer bottles littered the tables and filled the place's garbage cans to the brim. Suddenly the record changed and the bassy voice of "Mad Lion" came through the speakers prompting both the Afro-American and Jamaican women to scream with glee as they jumped out of their seats to their feet and performed a sexually and provocative dance called the "Wind". A man of medium height and weight, but a giant in drug sales, known as Dog,

Influenced by all the liquor he'd consumed, drunkenly wrapped his arm around the shoulders of another man who was just as equally drunk, and spoke loudly into his ears. From across the room, another man, oblivious to the loud-ear—shattering music, and the people bumping into him, kept his eyes on his prey. Watching the men hugging, seconds later he observed the man named Dog turn and muscle his way through the crowd of people on the dance floor.

Drunkenly, Dog stumbled into the deserted bathroom. Looking around him, he seen that the stand-up urines were too far away and decided to use one of the toilet booths since it was the closest to him. Inside the stall, preoccupied with the task of finding his zipper Dog hadn't bother to close the stall door and was totally unaware of the man who had entered the stall behind him. The alcohol, coupled with the compromising position he was in at the moment prevented him from reacting in time to stop the Ghetto Soldier from putting him in a full-nelson headlock. Dog dropped his hands to his sides thinking it to be a practical joke that he and his friend often played on one another, suddenly was taken aback when Junior's voice, a stranger's voice, whispered two questions in his ear.

The first question was: did he want to live? Not liking the answer to the second question which wasn't the forthcoming of information, the Ghetto Soldier applied more pressure around Dog's neck cutting off his air supply. When as if, with a six sense, he sensed that Dog wanted to comply, he released the pressure from around Dog's neck, yet only enough for him to speak, by this time, in a state of stupefied panic "Blade . . . Blade Diamond," Dog breathed, he then went on to give the other statistics. Immediately after having spilled his guts Dog felt shameful of his actions and then became angry with himself when the thoughts of his West Indian heritage, telling him that he was infallible entered his head. Dog's nose flared now with rage—replacing his fear. In a stupor, he grabbed a hold of one of the massive arms around his neck and attempted to break free. For this he was severely punished. Lifted off of his feet, Dog was slung around in the stall like a rag doll. His eyes bulged as if trying to pop out of their sockets, veins in his forehead poked out puffy against his skin as fleeting thoughts told him that this thing holding him was not—could not possibly be human.

The force around his neck which now felt like a vice, increased in pressure causing Dog's bowel to break, urine and feces ran down his pants legs. Seconds later Dog's neck snapped with a sickening sound—only he didn't hear it.

"Nighty-night Dog," the Ghetto Soldier whispered, sitting Dog up on the toilet seat, he leaned him back against the wall so he wouldn't fall.

The Ghetto Soldier emerged from the stall and found the bathroom still empty. Rejoining the people partying, he walked around the out-skirts of the people shaking their ass on the dance floor until he was exactly behind the second man he sought. Removing a nine inch ice pick from the sleeve of his black leather jacket, his huge hand covered the mouth of his prey as the ice pick sought, searched, found and then forced its way through the man's rib cage, puncturing his lungs in six different places. This had been done with such precision and speed that no one had seen a thing. When the hand covering the man's mouth dropped, he looked around in a daze but could not identify his attacker. Clutching his side now in total horror he tried to scream but failed as he choked on his own blood. No one paid much attention to the man as he fell to the floor—thinking he probably had too much to drink or that perhaps it was his way of dancing, and by the time anyone realized that it wasn't, the man wearing the black leather jacket had long since gone.

The time was 12:59 A.M. Infinite looked out his window for the second time, it was more like peeking out, as he pushed the curtain aside with one hand, with a .357 in the other. This posture flashed a picture on the screen in his mind of a poster he once seen of Malcolm-X who was posed pretty much the way he was now, with the exception that Malcolm-X was holding an AR-15 in his hand, and beneath this pose were the words: By Any Means Necessary. At the moment Infinite was more leery than afraid. He knew that tonight things were going to go down for certain people and there lay the fact that those who knew could have leaked it out to those it was going to happen to. And he wasn't taking any chances on a fool creeping up on him. In the next instant he seen a sparkling gray Lexus Coup come to a full stop in front of his house, "It's about time," he said out loud, indulging in self-talk.

Unique was blowing the horn for the second time as Infinite ran out the front door of his building and into the passenger seat. Upon seeing him Unique said, "Peace God!"

"Knowledge—knowledge," Infinite said adjusting his seat.

Infinite stood five feet eight; he had short hair and beady eyes that were always shifting. He had the type of persona that made people think he was a troublemaker, and those who thought this weren't wrong. "Damn, you took long enough God; you know we gotta get this thing done tonight,"

Infinite said, "You straight?"

"That's why I'm here."

"Aw'ight, then let's do this." As the Lexus pulled off a light torrid of rain began to pour. Unique flipped on the headlights and the windshield wipers. The Harlem streets were beginning to clear fast of the people walking on the streets. In contrast to Infinite's persona, he lived on a very quiet block on west 138th and Frederick Douglas Blvd, formerly known as 8th avenue. Unique drove down 8th avenue until he got to 155th street where he parked in front of a ball park across the street from the Polo Grounds projects. Close to fifteen guys were standing around on the Ruckus basketball court talking. Though the rain had stopped, their basketball laid in a puddle on the ground. The trees which bent over the top of the park's fence took away the lighting from the street lights. The sound of the Lexus door slamming caused the men to turn around. In the next instant Unique and Infinite both heard someone yell out, "Yo Inf' that's you?"

"I'm not gone keep telling you motherfuckers about yelling my name out in the streets," Infinite said as he walked further into the park. Flavor and Chico stepped out of the crowd and walked over to meet him and Unique. Raising his hand Flavor gave Infinite a pound, "What's up my nigga?"

"A nigga is an ignorant person—do I come across as stupid to you?" Infinite asked and then said, "Speak to me when you learn how to address a person with respect, for them as well as yourself Blackman."

"Oh, ah, pardon self Inf'," Flavor capped quickly, "My bad." Knowing that Infinite's temperament was truly unpredictable. Both Flavor and Chico focused in on Unique, "Nice whip you got there Unique. So what's up?" In response Unique nodded his head only.

"Who's all them people?" Infinite said point towards the ball court. "They ain't nobody," Flavor said, knowing what Infinite meant.

"They was here when we got here, "said Chico.

"Aw'ight, here's the science," Infinite said, "So do the knowledge. The money from the spot on one-four-nine was like only three gees, which is like three times less than usual. And this shit done happened three times already. According to my mathematics that's Wisdom Knowledge, borning, understanding, so we ain't barking no more—we biting."

"I know, I know," Flavor said nervously, knowing he did not want to be the one getting bit, "It's that motherfucker Blackseed cutting our throat—fucking up the flow man, I'm telling you, its gotta be".

"Yeah—word," Chico added, "After y'all spoke to us about it the last time we kept our eyes open—word to life. The cheat is in, only we don't know how he's doing it, but it ain't us man, and that's for sure."

Unique spoke up, "Well like I told him two nights ago—if my money was funny again it means he's still pushing dimes of his own shit, stopping the twenties. And I gave my word that I would squeeze some hot rocks up in a nigga's ass, and my word is bond, so that nigga got to go."

"Man," Infinite cut in not able to resist the opportunity to gas things up even more, "I don't believe that nigga think you'll do it. He don't think it can happen. Plus you wasn't even convincing enough the last time Uiee," Infinite instigated, "You know that nice, quiet voice you got seem to only work on the girls," to further explain his point he began to mimic the way Unique had spoke a night ago, in a soft quiet voice, "If my money ain't right tomorrow night Blackseed, I'ma kill you—word is bond."

"Yeah, well, it's the quiet motherfuckers like me you have to be careful of," Unique defended himself though knowing he didn't have to, "Besides, you motherfuckers is suppose to be on top of this shit, and I wouldn't have to!"

"Well check it," Flavor said, "Let's go count this cheddar now and if it ain't right," he pulled a .380 from his hip, "We'll make it right!"

"Yeah. Let's do that," Infinite said. The men piled into the Lexus and drove six blocks to 149th street. Parking the car between 148th and 147th, the four men walked into a tenement building that looked as though it should have been abandoned years ago.

When they reached a third floor apartment a very young black man recognizing them through the peephole let them in.

"Hot Tee, what's up?" Infinite said addressing the door man. Hot Tee was slim and brown skin with needle marks running down his arm. "Peace God," Hot Tee replied, "Love is love, know w' I mean?"

"Yeah, no doubt, now what's up with that trap?"

"Its right here God," Hot Tee said, "But business is kinda slow, as if the dopers done got cured or something, cause we ain't been getting no type of traffic." Infinite looked over at Unique, Flavor and Chico who were standing beside him listening to the conversation.

"Everybody let's sit down while I count this money," Infinite said. Although the drugs belonged to Unique, Infinite was the manager and head of security. Unique dropped down heavily on the dilapidated couch as if the gun in the center of his back weighed a ton and was weighing him down. Infinite reached into his pocket, pulled out a fifty dollar bill and gave it to Hot Tee, "Yo, go get us some Hydro, and some 40's of crazy-horse. But go get whatever work you got left first and bring it in here." Hot Tee disappeared in a room and returned with two large zip lock bags full of tiny squares of wax bags, each bag contained a pale light beige powdery substance—Heroin. He then handed Infinite a bundle of money. Taking the money Infinite exclaimed, "What the fuck is this? This is all the trap you got?"

"Ye, ye, yeah Inf'," stammered Hot Tee, "I told you shit was slow, damn, I'm sorry man. I was here all day—twelve hours, you can check with the "look out", he can tell you God, I swear, word is bond."

"Aw'ight, aw'ight, calm the hell down, shit. I ain't gone shoot you," Infinite said deceptedly, knowing the thought had crossed his mind.

Both flavor and Chico tried to hold back their laughter from the frightful expression on Hot Tee's face, but were failing terribly.

"I'm glad y'all find humor in this shit," Infinite said, "Cause if this money ain't correct y'all won't be getting paid tonight." At these words both men stop laughing. Infinite continued, "Yo Chico, let Hot Tee out and Tee, hurry back with the stimulation." Chico walked over to the door with Hot Tee behind him, looking through the peephole first; he quickly unlocked the door, Hot Tee slid out just as quickly. At this time Flavor was returning from one of the back rooms where he had found another worker by the name of Brice, who was sleeping in bed accompanied by two females who Flavor recognized from living in the hood. He knew Brice was probably the one who had stayed up all night and not Hot Tee. The men sat around the living room watching as Infinite pour out the contents in the zip lock bags on top of a makeshift coffee table, "Was Blackseed here?" he asked.

"I just spoke with Brice sleeping in the back," said Flavor, "And he said Blackseed was here all night and left a little while ago." Grunting, Infinite began counting the money, he counted a thousand dollars in tens, and twenty bills. He then counted the wax bags and was up to forty-six when Unique reached over into the pile and began counting with him, "Uiee, what the hell you doing?" Infinite asked.

"I'm counting up with you Gee, chill."

"The sun don't chill Allah, now put that shit down and let me do my job.

"You mean Blackseed's job?" Unique shot back.

Infinite mistakenly dropped a bag back into the pile, "Shit. Now look what you made me do, I fucking lost count."

"You know something Inf', you need to stop polluting the air with all your profanity.

"Ah shit," Infinite said, "Did Trisha tell you that? I had this broad who once told me some shit like that, that's some shit a broad would say. Yo, don't go turning wisdom on me God, word!"

"Ah, take care of your business," Unique said dropping the bags back on the table, feeling somewhat irritated that Infinite had put his finger on the fact that he had in fact took the saying from Trisha. Just as Infinite began his count again they all heard a knock at the door at the same time that they heard crackling sounds of static coming from both the police scanner and walkie-talkie laying on the kitchen table. Because everyone was already jumpy about being in the spot, everyone drew their gats simultaneously. Flavor's heartbeat was pounding in his ear, "Who's that?" He asked in a whisper.

"Ssshh. Quiet!" said Infinite, picking up the walkie-talkie he whispered, "Atomic Bomb, what's the deal?" The voice of the—look-out—man underneath the canopy on the roof came back clear over the walkie-talkie, "Everything's good. Raheem just gave me the signal that a customer's coming up for five, my bad."

"If the custy is coming up, then who the fuck is at the door?" Infinite said into the walkie-talkie.

"Hot Tee went in the building a few seconds before the customer with a bag in his hand, so it's probably him." Everyone breathed a sigh of relief. "Damn, that was quick. Yo Chico, get the door man." Chico went to answer the door with his gat in his hand. Hot Tee walked in carrying a bag full of beer. Before he could set it down, Flavor jumped up and slammed Chico's head, face first against the wall and relieved him of the gat in his waist, "Motherfucker, if you ever open the fucking door again without first looking through the peephole and I'm in this motherfucker, I'll kill you. You hear me, word, I'll kill you!"

"Yo, get the fuck off me," Chico yelled.

"Yo! Yo! Infinite shouted, pulling Flavor up off of Chico. "First off, shut the fucking door." Chico was putting all the locks back on the door when Infinite spun on him, "You was wrong Chico for opening the door

Without using precaution first, how many times we told you the importance of the peephole?" Without waiting for a response he turned to Flavor, "And you, you shouldn't have jumped on him like that. Man it's hard to believe that you two are cousins." Unique looked at the smile on Infinite's face, and thought he was such a hypocrite, no matter how much he tried to hide it he liked shit like that.

"You're right," Flavor said, "I'm sorry Chico."

"Yo, forget it; I still got mad love for you."

"Aw'ight, now let's get this other shit right, I got a thousand dollars in cash right here, which means we only suppose to have four hundred and fifty bags left, yet we got seven hundred and fifty bags left. So can somebody tell me where the fuck the rest of these bags came from?" Everyone looked at each other.

"That motherfucker!" Unique jumped up barking, "It's Blackseed, fucking Blackseed, that nigga's gonna be ghost cause its drama. Aw'ight, here's the deal, we all heard at one time or another that that nigga is trying to do something on 127th and 8th. So we're all gonna creep down there and catch his punk ass, but I'm the one whose gonna push his shit back!"

"Hey, hey, wait, that's my j—"

"Naw-naw Inf'," Unique said, "I gotta do this. My word is my bond and I'll die before my word shall fail."

"Fuck it, aw'ight, let's do it."

Brice was awaked from his sleep before the men left. When the men reached the ground floor of the building Infinite gave Hot Tee two hundred dollars, "You did good baby, be here tomorrow morning before eleven."

"Aw'ight, peace Gods!"

"Peace." The four men said simultaneously stepping out into the night. Music could be heard blasting from a car's stereo half way up the block. The lyrics reached them as they walked in its direction: "I was in the jeep tinted with heat/beats bumping/across the street/you was wilding-talking/'bout how you was running the Island in 89/laying up/playing the yard with crazy shine/I said fuck that/this was gravy nigga/it's mines!"

"It's a beautiful night for a homicide—let's ride," Infinite said as they neared Unique's Lexus. Just then someone started shouting, "Yo Inf'! Yo Inf'!" The men turned around. "Who the hell is that?" Asked Unique not able to see in the dark.

"I don't know but I done told motherfuckers 'bout yelling my name out like that."

"Yo that's Raheem," said Flavor.

"Ah shit, he wants' to get paid. Yo Chico, go give him this hundred before the nigga break his neck getting over here," Infinite said, seeing Raheem still walking fast towards them and yelling but the loud music coming from the black BMW with tinted windows prevented them from hearing from hearing him.

"And tell that bird to stop yelling out my name."

Suddenly the black BMW came racing down the street with the music still blaring, "You better watch them niggas that be close to you/and make sure they do what they suppose to do/cause thems the niggas who be thinking 'bout smoking you/never personal now-a-days it's just business."

When the BMW pulled alongside of the Lexus with its window rolled down the men all seen the glitter of chrome flashing bright in the darkness of the night. Infinite reacted first, "It's a hit!" He yelled bailing for the ground. Suddenly the music in the car died out and someone yelled, "SEED NIGGAS . . . WHAT?" Preceded by gunshots fired from the car's window causing the night to come alive with cries and screams from women and children running for cover on the crowded block.

Unique, Infinite and Flavor had already ducked behind a car and was now firing back at the BMW as it sped away with its rear window shattered. Suddenly Flavor began shouting and screaming, "NO! NO! NO! THEY KILLED CHICO! I'MA MURDER THE BASTARDS! LOOK YO . . . THEY KILLED CHICO! THEY KILLED CHICO! AH MAN, THEY KILLED MY COUSIN!" Walking a few yards back down the block the men found it was true as they seen Chico lying on the ground in a puddle of his own blood. He only had half of a head now; the other side was mangled from where the bullet had struck. Unique's hand holding his gat was shaking, only not from fear but rage as he looked down at Chico, who, though he had never mention before, reminded him of his little brother, whom he would not let hustle for this very reason. But he was no fool and knew that his younger brother was somewhere doing his own thing, and quite well, if the rumors that he heard were true.

CHAPTER THREE

Hours ago Junior Washington had enjoyed himself in the company of his family; his wife Karla, his daughter Kim, and his brother Daryle. Their quality time had begun that morning at I-Hop, where they ate a hardy breakfast. From there they shoved off to Rye Play land where everyone had transformed into little kids again under the influence of excitement. Everyone allowed the gypsy to read their fortune except Junior. Karla had taken notice of this. They played water sport games of shooting water into the clown's mouth where both Junior and Daryle had won several prizes. When they reached the rifle range, the aim of both Kim and Karla seemed far superior to Junior and Daryl's, which enabled them to win far more stuffed animals than the men. Intuitively, however, Karla had gotten the impression it was based on chivalry. They ate burgers and hot dogs for lunch and filled up on a lot of carbohydrates. Bloated from all the junk food they left the amusement park and drove to the Science Observation Deck located right off route 9W. When they began to see stars every time they closed their eyes they decided it was time to go. From there they wound up at the doors of the Museum of African Arts; the exhibits left them yearning with a desire to learn more about their family tree.

Their departure from the museum led them to pounder where Man was headed. They had dinner a few blocks away on 45th and Broadway at the All Star Café that boast a bar on the second floor and a diner on the third. Their night ended about half a mile from home at a park called Wingate. Free concerts were held there every summer with performances by notable celebrities. The concert had ended as of two hours ago and Junior Washington had taken his family home.

He now stood inside a multi-complex car garage on Roger Avenue. Although there were several cars and vehicles in this garage he owned and could choose from, for tonight's occasion he chose a black minivan that was fully stocked with state-of-the-art equipment. He stood in front of it now placing a black, flight Pan Am bag in the back. The weather was truly hot outside and the confines of the garage made it even hotter, and the bullet proof vest he had on beneath his sweatshirt didn't make matters any better. However, he was used to heat—heat of the worse kind. The hotter it was the better he performed. He had conditioned his body to withstand and endure pressure under the most adverse conditions. The black knitted skull cap on his head served a dual purpose; it was also a ski mask.

The garage at this time was deserted as Junior, sitting behind the steering wheel of the van made a last minute check on his Walter PK19 hanging from a thatch, concealed beneath his jacket. He then fasten the snaps on the sheaf of the Bowie-Knife strapped to his ankle.

As the black minivan pulled out the garage and onto the streets, the Pursuit 2000 night-vision glasses on Junior Washington's face suddenly enabled his vision to zoom further ahead on the road.

*   *   *

The black clad figure moved noiselessly through the darkness of the night and onto the roof of a garage in a backyard, and then through a gangway leading to the front of a house. Crossing the street he entered another gangway that led him to another backyard, and finally to the garage he'd been looking for. Squatting to his knee he reached into a small pouch on his waist, removing a file and hook, he began picking the lock at the bottom right hand corner of the garage door.

Less than a minute later he noiselessly made his way into the garage. The beam of his pen flashlight spotted a white BMW parked along side of a black Volvo. In back of the Volvo sat a gold 300E Mercedes Benz. He was moving between these cars when the pen flashlight slipped from between his lips and fell to the ground, he had it there so that either of his hands could be free in the event of a sneak attack by a dog. He froze in his step, holding his breath, his ears perked up to access if his unlawful entry had been detected. Several seconds later when he heard nothing he exhaled, and bent down to pick up the pen light when his eyes caught sight of a silver-spur Rolls Royce parked in the far corner of the garage. It was beautiful, the best he'd ever seen. Shining the light into the back window he saw a wet-bar, telephone, a Nintendo Game console, a miniature TV. and a VCR with the Scarface video sitting on top.

Moving away, he checked to see if there was an alarm on the second garage door which led into the house. Finding none, the black clad figure, using hook and file again, gained entry to the Five hundred thousand dollar house. The numbers on the front of the house read: 15 Deanno Court, located in the exclusive community of Dix Hills, in the county of Suffolk. In the house, he slowly moved about from a kitchen that was fully stocked. Next to the kitchen was a small room that housed a State-of-the-Art gym. Reaching the living room, the first thing he noted was the 56 inch screen TV. The spacious living room walls, as well as the walls along the staircase which lead to the bedrooms upstairs were graced with paintings that looked authentic. There were two bathrooms, both with sunken tubs the size of small swimming pools, there was also a sauna and steam room. The carpet on the steps along the hallway allowed him to move noiselessly, from room to room, down the corridor to the Master bedroom.

Removing one of the tech 10's from beneath his arms and into a viable position, he pocketed the pen light as he approached the threshold of the door that was already partly ajar. From his position he could see the bedroom light was turned off. Taking no chances, he placed his back against the hallway wall and peeked into the room with two quick jerks before he was satisfied. He then entered the room stopping just inside with both techs in his hand, pointing towards the ceiling Academy style while his eyes adjusted to the darkness. As his pupils dilated he was able to make out more clearly the shape of a body lying in the bed underneath the covers. He was grateful there was only one body. His adrenaline caused the blood pumping through his veins to move faster and his heartbeat to quicken as he realized he'd finally found one of the two link's in the chain that had tried to strangle the life out of his family.

Finally here, he feared that something would still go wrong as he listen to the rise and fall of the person breathing in bed. Slowly, cautiously, Junior Washington approached the bed and nudged the temple of the man with the choker-muzzle screwed onto the tip of the tech. The feel of the cold blue steel made Blade Diamond jump up out of his sleep into a sitting position, "What the fuck," was all he managed to get out before a gloved hand covered his mouth. And it was at this moment that Blade Diamond believed he was having a nightmare, a bad dream, it had to be. And the more reality sat in the more he realized it was. He wondered how it could be, how could anyone have bypassed the alarm on the windows and both the front and back doors. His breathing became laborish as his mouth dried from fear when he sensed the chilled premonition of death reflecting in the eyes behind the mask on the face breathing down on him, so close he could feel his breath on his skin. The eyes seemed illuminated by the window light. They were chilling. Horrifying. He couldn't help but to notice the contrast between the body heat coming from the mask man and the dead, menacing, cold touch of the gun now pressed against his throat. Releasing Blade Diamond's mouth, the gloved hand harshly grabbed him by the collar of his pajama and dragged him from the bed. "Whoa . . . what do you want?" Blade Diamond gurgled, "Who are you?" . . . What do you want with me?" Deciding to show he wasn't stupid he said, "I know . . . . I know . . . You want money, right?" Okay . . . Okay—take it . . . easy man," he managed to get out before the gloved hand strangled and choked off his words, making them sound as if he had sucked in air from a helium balloon and was now trying to talk. On all fours, Blade Diamond crawled to the far right side of the room, reaching the wall which held a large painting of the Exotic Goddess in the Nude; he pulled back a corner of the carpet on the floor which revealed a safe built into the parquet floor. Opening its door Blade Diamond quickly tried to reach inside. For that, he was immediately punished with a slap against the bridge of his nose from one of the Tech's and then was forced to lay face down. Removing a small, black tie string bag from his waist, then Junior filled it with the contents from the safe. He counted thirty-five stacks of hundred dollar bills that looked to have at least a hundred bills in each stack, and a miniature draw string suede black bag that held fifteen D-flawless diamonds in it. He also removed two pearl handle .380 handguns. This done, he tied Blade Diamond's hands behind his back. "Whoa . . . what you doing? Blade Diamond's voice croaked, "You got the money and everything . . . . Why are you still bothering me? Oh God! Leave me alone! . . . What do you want from me?" He cried as he was being gagged with a pillow case and another pulled over his head. He felt himself being pulled up from the floor as Junior lead him down the stairs and out of the house.

Blade Diamond grunted when his body met the full impact of the van's floor. Forced into a sitting position his hands were tied to a steel ring inside the van. He bumped his head against the van's wall as it drove along the streets. Blade Diamond had no idea who had abducted him, why, or where they were going.

They had been riding for at least two hours, Blade Diamond noted as he tried to connect the cold eyes behind the mask with a face. When the van finally stopped he tried to talk but the gag in his mouth prevented any comprehensible communication. The sweat of fear soaked his silk pajamas causing it to cling to his body. When he was removed from the van he perked up his ears for sounds that would clue him in to where he was at, but the only sounds he heard was the soft click of the van's door sliding closed before he was shoved and then dragged into a building and up four flights of stairs.

He recognized the smell along the way, it was the smell of rot, mildew, as he was lead through what he imagined was an apartment he tripped over the debris on the floor and would have fell several times had it not been for his captor holding him tightly by the arm. He had been forced to sit down in what felt like a wooden chair. He tilted his head to one side listening again for sounds to give him a clue. He jumped and started when he felt his hands behind him being untied.

He then heard a raucous, chilling voice instructing him to remove the pillowcase and the gag. The first thing he recognized when his eyes focus was Junior Washington standing in front of him with a big ugly gun pointed at his face. The second thing he noticed which confirmed his suspicion was that they were indeed inside a condemned building, but where he didn't know. As he speculated on this his thoughts were interrupted, "Stand up and take off your clothes, and I mean everything, I want you butt ass naked."

Doing as he had been instructed the nervousness in Blade Diamond's voice proved that he was truly scared. "Do I know you from somewhere? Da-did I do something wrong to offend you my man?" He asked trying desperately to control the tremor in his voice. "I don't recall ever doing anything wrong to you. You already got my money and everything—what more do you want from me my brother?"

It seemed that these last words angered his abductor and he received a blow to the face which on impact knocked over the chair.

"I ain't your brother motherfucker," Junior spat.

"Okay—okay broth—, I mean man," Blade diamond said from the floor with an arm in the air to ward of the blow he anticipated would be coming for his blunder. "You got that . . . just please, don't hit me no more, please, you ain't gotta do that, I'm doing what you want, whatever you want please!" He said getting up from the floor totally naked sitting back down in the chair.

"That's right fool," Junior uttered through clench teeth, "and since you're in a begging mood, put your hands in a prayer's position. No, not like that, behind your back." Doing as instructed Blade Diamond felt his hands being tied again behind him. He was really scared now; the more he realized it the more it seemed to heighten, frightening him out of his wits. The fact that he was naked made him feel even more vulnerable. He remembered reading somewhere that the psychological effect of being naked made the captive feel despair and helpless, and from the situation he now found himself in, he tended to agree. He watched as his abductor remove a rope from a dust bag on the floor. This was used to tie him to the chair. His abductor then walked around in front of him, "Yeah Scram Jones, I've been waiting a long time for this moment."

"Watcha mean man . . . . Whatcha mean?" Blade whined, his fear had taken over completely now, "You want money? . . . Is that it? . . . That's it right? You want more money. Okay, I'll give you more money, okay? . . . You want a boat? . . . I got a yacht! And it's yours my man. You can have it all. Just please, OH JESUS, PLEASE don't kill me. Let me live . . . I won't tell a soul . . . . In exchange for my life . . . I SWEAR!"

"Your sorry ass should have thought about that when you took advantage of that woman and her little girl."

"What—, I, d—," speaking so quickly Blade Diamond choked on his saliva, he coughed, 'What woman? What little girl? Brother you're mistaking me for somebody else," he spoke quickly; "I ain't hurt no woman, and I would never hurt no kid. I love children; I have three of my own. Let's talk about this brother, there's been a mistake, ain't no need for us to be acting like savages brothers." Blade was admonished again, this time, punched in the eye with a blow that made him see stars and immediately swell close. The jarring, thumping, excruciating pain pounding in his head now made him become instantly religious, "OH GOD . . . OH GOD! OH GOD! You're killing me . . . . AHHHHH HA, ha, ha, ha . . . Please GOD Save me!" The volume of Blade's cry caused him to be gagged again. And each of his legs was tied at the ankle to the legs of the chair.

Junior's watch told him it was now three o'clock in the morning. Reaching into his back pocket he removed a straight razor, its chrome steel blade glistening in the dark caused Blade Diamond's heart to drop, and he grunted. It was more of a moan as he realized the kind of damage that the barber's razor could do. Junior now walked towards him, "That woman you took advantage of . . . she's my wife," the Ghetto Soldier hissed, emphasizing each word as the razor sliced into the flesh of Blade Diamond's chest, face, and arms. "And that little girl, that thirteen year old girl . . . . that you . . . and your goons . . . molested . . . is my daughter . . . . My only daughter . . . . She was in a trauma ward . . . . for nearly a year . . . . because you raped . . . . and sodomized her . . . motherfucker!" Slashed Junior. Each word was met by a thrust, repeatedly, over and over again, "Raped . . . . Sodomized . . . Molested . . . Crazy House . . . Trauma ward!"

Blade Diamond strained against his confines in the chair with only his one eye to convey all he felt.

Tired of this Junior dropped the razor, Blade's red blood shined bright in contrast as it dripped from Junior's tight, black leather glove. Reaching into the bag again he pulled out a bottle of ammonia and another plastic bag that was filled with salt from the sea. He then began pouring salt from the bag into the wounds on Blade Diamond's body. The extent of pain this caused made him slam back against the chair with such force that both it and him keel over to the floor. Hovering, Junior dropped the empty bag on top of top of him. "How does it feel Blade to have someone put salt in your game?" Junior said, sitting his chair back up straight. Blade was afraid to speak until he seen through his one open eye the ammonia bottle in Junior's hand and him now pouring it into his open wounds. He shut his eye tight upon contact in hopes it would somehow stop the oncoming pain, but it didn't.

Blade Diamond regained consciousness sometime later, and heard the chilling, but now familiar voice taunting him. At first it sounded like it was coming from far away. "Karla . . . that's her name. Karla. You remember her don't you Blade? And of course you remember her daughter Lady, right? . . . Kim? . . . my daughter?" As Blade's eye became focus on the black clad figure standing in front of him something triggered in his mind, perhaps it was the names he'd just heard, he began connecting those names to faces, but it was hard since it was so long ago. Karla, he could see her face now in his mind, and then her body . . . he also remembered her daughter . . . . this mad man's daughter. Silently he cursed the day he had been introduced to her by that young crack head kid name Daryle.

Silently, the Ghetto Soldier walked across the room towards something, and when he removed a dust cloth Blade seen it was a generator, through his one open eye he seen the mad man also pull out what looked like a Black & Decker drill. His eye followed the cord to the generator and seen that it extended outside the window. He surmised it was somehow connected to the light pole in the backyard. This told him that this whole thing had been pre-arranged, premeditated. His thoughts were then intruded upon. "Karla . . . my wife, gave birth to a three pound, two ounce baby. She didn't even know who the father was due to all the men she slept with to support her crack habit. But the baby died, it didn't survive, maybe that baby was yours Mr. Blade Diamond?"

The dryness from fear had caused Blade's throat to shrink even more. This was the first time that this mad man addressed him by his full name with such familiarity, unlike a stranger would have done.

"I know you're sorry now for what you did to her—aren't you?" The mad man asked as he walked towards him now with the drill twirling in his hand. Blade Diamond, frantic now, shook his head, hysterically, from side to side as he sat stuck in his chair. The first hole Junior made was in Blade's kneecaps. The nerve ending pain of the steel bit drilling through his bones without a sedative had pushed him closer to the edge of insanity. Pulling the bit out now, Junior began to make a game out of drilling a hole into Blade's chin, "This little piggy went to the crack house . . . and this little piggy stayed home." The grinding of the drill-bit biting into Blade's chin made his body go into convulsions, where he jerked uncontrollably. The withdrawal of the bit from his chin sponsored a pain that forced Blade Diamond back into unconsciousness. As he slipped back into darkness his last thought was that he was not going to make it out of here alive. He hoped the mad man would just kill him and get it over with so he wouldn't have to deal with the agony of pain. But something told him that that was the purpose of the mad man's performance.

When he regained consciousness sometime later he heard the voice in the dark ask, "Who is your connect?" He noted that the voice seemed even further away this time, the second thing he noted was the duck tape had been ripped from his mouth. "I asked you a question."

"PLEASE . . . . PLEASE . . . . PLEASE!" Blade pleaded with a weak voice, ignoring the question in hopes it would egg the man on to finish him off. Thinking that in this stupor Blade Diamond hadn't heard him Junior walked closer to him and quietly screamed into his face, "Motherfucker, you got a hearing problem? I asked you who do you get your work from?"

Blade tried to spit in Junior's face but was so weak the spittle ran down his own chin.

"Oh, so you wonna play tough, huh?" Junior reached into the small dust bag again and pulled out a spool of nylon fishing line. Walking over to a closet door in the apartment he tied one end of the line around the open closet door doorknob. The spool rolled out, though taunt, as he walked back over to where Blade was sitting. He then tied the other end of the fishing line tightly around Blade's shrivel manhood and nut sack. This done, he stood up wiping the dirt from the knees of his pants. "Now I'm going to ask you just once more. Whose your connect?" When Blade did not respond, Junior walked over to the open door. Just then Blade realized what the mad man was going to do, just the thought of it alone was painful, and he stumbled over his words in attempt to speak, "I, ah, no, wait." Junior's hand grabbing the door opened it even more, and then slammed it shut, causing the fishing line to cut deep into the skin of Blade Diamond's testicles. A horrifying scream ripped from his lips and then died as his head slump to his chest.

A half hour later Blade Diamond came to with no idea how long he had been out this time. At first he thought he had perhaps died, until he opened his eye and seen the mad man leaning against the generator. The look of death in this man's eyes caused him to reflect back on the spectrum of his life. On the screen of his mind he saw his wife, and his three daughters, who were at their grandparents for the weekend. His heart soared realizing he would never see them again. But then again . . . He hoped.

"Ah, I see you're back with us," Junior Washington said approaching. At this moment the thought occurred to Blade that this man might spare his life if he told him what he wanted to know. After all, it seemed to be the only thing he was now interested in. Blade spoke up weakly, "If . . . if I told you what you want to know . . . will you . . . let me go . . . be with my family?"

"You ain't in no position to be bargaining motherfucker. Now do you have a name and address for me? Or do we have to go through this whole thing all over again? I'm quite sure you're aware that I don't mind, know what I mean?"

"Please . . . don't kill me," Blade heard himself saying, "I want to live . . . I want to see my family again . . . so I'll tell you whatever you want to know."

"I want to know your connect and where he can be found," Junior said squatting down in front of him.

"It's . . . it's an Italian guy out in Green Point, Brooklyn, and named Johnny. He's got a black partner named Cut, he's the guy I use to do business with, I been out of the game for some time now."

"Tell me more," said Junior.

An hour later the Ghetto Soldier had all the information he needed and had no further use for Blade Diamond, who was now gagged again. Forced to stand from the chair with his hands still tied behind him, Junior Washington made him walk backwards. He never saw the hole he stepped into in the floor behind him. As Blade Diamond fell, Junior called down after him, "Say hello to my little friends."

Blade Diamond fell from the fourth floor to the third, through the third to the second. His body lingered half way in and half way out of the first floor landing hole before toppling over into the basement where he landed on a tattered, lice infested mattress, which happened to be the nest haven for a pact of mangy dogs that had rabies. They were so hungry that their rib cage showed visibly, poking through their matted mane of hair. Eight pairs of glowing red eyes focused in on Blade Diamond in the dark. The two dogs nearest him growled, baring their bacteria teeth. Foams of dribble drool down their mouth as the rest of them whined from hunger pain. Seconds later, the dogs, setting in for the feast attacked Blade Diamond's body like a pack of wolves slaughtering a lamb . . . . for to them he was!

CHAPTER FOUR

Twenty-five year old Daryle Washington, brother of Junior Washington, thought of himself as a young black prince; and a success just waiting to happen. Through a bout with fate he had almost been permanently taken out of the happy race of acquiring milk and honey, but through the help of his older brother had bounced back—and intact. Having once been addicted to crack, he believed he'd met the bottomless pits of hell, and only through the grace of God, and the one choice ultimatum his brother had given him, had managed to drag his ass back to the real world. From his experience though, he believed he had been in a war, a war much worse than Vietnam and Desert Storm combined. And had survived. He knew what living in the eternal hellfire was all about, because for five years he had lived there for every waking minute of his life—even in his sleep he dreamed about crack.

Now he was out to get all the things that life had to offer. Not only did he stop smoking crack but he no longer sold it. His only vice now was weed. With the money his brother had given him as a means of staying out of trouble, Daryle had acquired a recording studio and started up his own production company. Because he wanted Puff Daddy, Steve Stout, Jermaine Dupree and all the other producers to know he was now on the set, Daryle was always looking for new talent.

Although now a business man, his character displayed that he still had a lot of streets in him, which to him was a plus because it kept him up on what was going down in them.

Daryle had the type of face that made a person look, and then look again, only the second time with interest. It had happened to him so often that he pretended not to notice anymore. He was young, and single because he hadn't met a woman yet who could throw on the spice to make him want to come home at night—no matter how good she looked or the tricks she could perform in bed. His attempts at relationships had always ended in a clash of their personalities. The bottom line was that he had too much individuality for them. Yet his, "I-don't-give-a-fuck" attitude seemed to be the very thing that attracted women to him, oppose to beating their feet in the opposite direction.

Although he had a room at his brother's house, he rarely stayed there. Though, as part of their agreement, he was forced to work out with his brother at least three days a week. He wore his shirts unbutton most of the time which gave him the chance to show off his six pack. His hair was short and wavy and he sported a diamond stud earring in his left ear. His even white teeth shined brightly against the lips of his cocoa brown skin.

Daryle didn't like his name as a promoter, thinking it was too plain. And his niece Kim, known as Lady, was campaigning with him to find a new one. He loved his niece; they had a lot in common regardless of the fact that she was seven years younger than him. They hung out a lot, so much that people not knowing the facts thought they went together. Kim . . . Lady was like his advisor who he always consulted with when it came to women, who mostly were her friends. Kim told him what ones to go out with and which to leave alone. Clues to which of them would shell out on the first night and which of them wouldn't. In Kim's eyes her uncle Daryle could do no wrong, and her friends learned this early on.

Daryl's White Ranger Rover sat parked in the back section of the parking lot on the grounds of the Galaxy Hotel on Pennsylvania Avenue, in East New York. He had recently returned from the "Boys to Men" concert out at Darien Lake's Performing Arts Center that featured 'Mya', 'Next', 'Uncle Sam', and 'Destiny's Child'. While there he had met a female, and like all groupies, she was in awe of celebrities. Through conversation he learned she was from Bedford

Stuyvesant in Brooklyn, and had drove their with some of her girlfriends. He also learned that though he wasn't a celebrity she was still in awe of him, and after the show had asked if she could ride back with him, to which he agreed.

The windows of the hotel room they were in allowed Daryle to look out and check on his SUV at any time. At the moment he was exiting the bathroom with nothing but a towel wrapped around his waist. He looked down at the girl on the bed musingly, his having just taken a shower should have clued her in that the show was over yet she hadn't caught the hint. To the average guy's standards the enchanting female would have been considered pretty and fun to be with, but to Daryle she was only a party to the game. His belief was that she was only with him because he was someone to be with, and had he been nobody she wouldn't have been with him. Although he tried to conceal it his face showed he was becoming a bit impatient with the pre-arranged plan he often made with his niece, which at the moment hadn't come through yet. She was supposed to have beeped him twenty minutes ago under the pretense that something drastic had happened and required his attention and presence, which would then give him the excuse needed to dump the chick and split the scene. The room had been rented for four hours and they'd already been in there for three.

Laying in bed, the young woman named Connie yawned and then stretched her succulent, long legs wide, "Why you go take a shower Daryle? You said you rented us this room for twenty-four hours so we have all night lover!"

Daryle, feeling he had already spent more time with her than he actually intended to, said, "Yeah, I know—it's just a perk of mine," he crooned, now spreading out on the bed next to her, "After sex I like to feel fresh all over again."

"You are always fresh," Connie teased, ruffling the waves in his hair.

"Yo, chill, what I told you about doing that shit," he said grabbing her wrist.

"Why you so conceit Daryle?" Connie smiled.

"I'm not conceit, I'm convinced."

"And what are you so convinced about?"

"That I'm today's answer and tomorrow's question!" He said rolling over to his side of the bed where he took a pack of Newports from his pants laying in a chair and lit one.

"Ooooo, you're so conceit! Connie drew out in a long breath. Wondering what was taking Kim so long, he seen his beeper hanging out of his pants pocket, and inconspicuously, thump the button off and then back on. This automatically made the beeper ring. He picked it up and looked into the screen that said nothing but pretended that it did, and reached for the phone thinking of the number to a pay phone he once use to call.

"What's wrong with your beeper?"

"What you mean?"

"Why's it ringing like that? It sounds funny."

"I don't know," Daryle lied, "It's probably the battery going dead." Just as he was about to dial the number his beeper rung off again, this time for real. He looked at the screen and seen it was Kim, he silently breathed a sigh of relief and then called her. He held the phone slightly away from his ear allowing Connie to hear what was being said. She listened to the conversation. "Yeah, what's up? Yeah? . . . word? When? That's fucked up—word! Yeah alright, don't go nowhere, I'm on m way right now. Alright, bye." He hung up and turned around to face Connie, "Damn, sorry yo, but some shit just happened, so there's a change of plan cause I gotta go," he concluded rolling out of the bed reaching for his clothes.

"What you mean you gotta go? Don't be trying to play me like no chicken-head Daryle!"

"What the fuck you're talking 'bout? Listen . . . I just told you something came up and I gotta get there. So you can lay here if you want until I get back or you can get dressed and I'll drop you off home or where ever it is you wonna go—the choice is yours."

Considering this Connie asked, "What time you're coming back?"

"I don't know, this is some real serious shit, it might take all night."

Connie remained silent as she contemplated this. At this same time Daryle surmised that if she made the wrong choice, he could just envision her, the expression that would be on her face when management came knocking on the door telling her that her time was up.

"I want to stay—but naw, you can take me home if you promise you'll call me as soon as you get through with your business?"

"I promise. Now hurry up and get dressed."

*　　*　　*

A tall black man who went by the name of Blackseed, stood in the middle of the block he had carved out for himself, a black bag dangled from his shoulder. The five men standing around gave their full attention. They were all aware of the coup he had attempted to pull last week on the guys he use to work for. They also knew he had killed one of them also, and knew he wasn't playing. Since that time he had been hitting them off with drug packages, and now the block was flooded with only their drugs. From the looks of things nobody else on the block wanted any trouble, except for his rivals, who, in retaliations to what he had done, came through the block a few nights ago in cars and shot the block up, only nobody got hurt aside from those who wanted to become a statistic.

With the emotionally moving voice of a preacher who spooled the gospel from a cold walk-in flat to his congregation, Blackseed shouted revelations to his men: "The time is now!" The time to rise up and above all these player haters who don't want us to be innovators! So, now, if you players wonna get dough—then let's get dough. But if not, then lay down and fold, cause I ain't taking no prisoners. This is my livelihood . . . your livelihood. This is how we eat! . . . This is where we eat. Now Unique, Infinite, that bitch ass nigga Flavor and the rest of them soft ass niggas whose suppose to be Gods, is gonna try and test the waters, our waters! So I'm giving y'all these gats here to get your player game on track and not get your wigs pushed back," Blackseed said handing out guns he pulled from his shoulder bag. He had planned to pull a Khadafy move long before he had gotten with Unique and Infinite. But he knew he had to first get to know his enemies strength and weaknesses before he could engage them in war. And what better way to study your enemy than from the inside, so he had joined them. The first thing he knew he had to do was gain their trust, and secondly, their dependency on him making sure that their operation ran smoothly. This done, he then purchased a stamp with the name that they were using on their product, and he then unknown to them began putting his own drugs out on their street and in their spot. It was only when they began to get suspicious did he know it what time to make his move. He also thought it clever on his part to approach the crooked cop name Pataki who was on Unique and Infinite's payroll, for the services of informing them when the block was due to be raided.

Recognizing the larceny in the cop, Blackseed knew it would be a cinch when he propositioned the cop for the same services that was rendered to Unique and Infinite. The cop would be receiving two envelopes now instead of one. Blackseed then knew that the only two people who were really posing a threat to his existence and his cash flow was Unique and Infinite, once they were out of the way everyone else would fall in line.

CHAPTER FIVE

It was 12:35 in the afternoon when a shiny white, four doors Q Infinity SUV, with smoky tinted windows, made its way off the expressway exiting on to Targee Street in Staten Island. It stopped at the red light as the young driver behind the wheel popped in his favor rap CD, adjusted the rearview mirror and then proceeded to spark flames to the blunt now hanging from his mouth. He had wanted to light it back in Rome, NY, but didn't want to risk the chance of getting pulled over and then be taken in for something petty. The expressway exit light turned green, the driver continued down Targee Street and then made a right turn up Sobel Court, and the street was lined with project buildings.

This young driver was very familiar with this area and these projects; in fact he knew them like he did the back of his hand. It was where he grew up but since then had moved on to other places; it was still the place he called home. Stopping momentarily at a stop sign, he observed the everyday hustlers who claimed the corners of Park hill and Sobel Court, doing their thing, clocking their grit. It put a smile on his face as he realized he hadn't seen these sights in close to seven weeks now. Making a left turn at the intersection, Jahborn, a neighborhood drug dealer, turned the CD player up to its maximum volume to avoid hearing people call him on the streets upon seeing his vehicle. Cruising slowly down the block he took inventory of both the new and old faces, as well as the activities that at the moment seemed to be the same as usual.

He pulled up to his destination, a bright red edifice with the figures '185' in big bold numbers which hung just below the building's front entrance. It was the place which had provided him with shelter for many years. The foundation from which he had first started his small enterprise. Double parking beside a white BMW, which clued him to the fact that the people he sought was in residence, he became excited. On the opposite side of the street he observed a few Jamaicans who, before his trip upstate, had tried to offer him some resistance over the type of drugs they were permitted to sell in his section of Park hill. The Jamaicans had originally started out selling weed to which he felt was cool since he smoked trees. But when they moved on to selling crack, without the decency of even making their product better than his, he'd given them a warning to dead it and sell weed only. When this warning had been ignored Jahborn had sent out his junior hit squad, and several days later when his rivals found one of their brethren's dead and his body filled with bullet holes his message became clear.

Jahborn, who was short, light skin and stocky, maintained his monster, gangster glare as he jumped out of his car with his blunt still burning. He ignored the Jamaicans presence as if they weren't there, yet he knew better than to sleep on them also. His jean shorts sagged far below his waist which showed off his thirty dollar designer boxer underwear's. He yelled up to one of the projects window with a shrilling "Yo!" The smoke from the blunt in his mouth hung in the air over his head. When he didn't get a response he hollered even louder this time, "Yo!" A few seconds later after still not getting a response, he turned to climb back into his car and peeked the Jamaicans looking in his direction but not at him, yet at him. Just then he heard a "Yo!" which came from a fourth floor window, "What's up my nigga?" Another young man called down to him.

"Everything is everything," he yelled back up.

"When you get back?"

"Just now. Come downstairs nigga—what the fuck!"

"I'm coming—I'm coming down now."

"Hurry up! Jahborn said. The blunt he had been smoking was now close to being a roach and he dropped it, reached into his car and grabbed another one out of the ashtray that was already rolled. He then leaned against the railing of the building a few feet away from his car and sparked flames to his new blunt while he waited for his long time friend and partner A.W., which was short for Always Weeded, to come down stairs. He was several drags into the blunt of Raspberry Cush weed when two crack heads from the projects approached him, "Hi Jahborn."

"What's up Jahborn?"

"The sun, moon, and the stars. What's the dealy yo?"

"You holding Jahborn?"

"Why? What's up? What you need?"

"I need two fifty pieces of that shit—can you help me?" The crack head named Shirley asked. She was a veteran fiend who had been his most loyal customer when he first got started in the business back in the early 80's. Though over a decade had passed, she was still smoking crack. Shirley held out her dirty hand with two crumbled fifty dollar bills.

"Somebody's coming down now who'll fix that order for you," he said leaning back against the rail puffing on his blunt.

"How long I gotta wait Jahborn? I got people at my house who sent me out for this." Before he could respond the lobby door swung open and A.W. stepped out, four thick gold chains dangled from his neck. He had on a burgundy tank top, and burgundy short jeans which also hung below his waist, and a blunt was stuck behind his ear.

"What's up my nigga?" He said sticking out his hand giving Jahborn a pound. Jahborn dropped the two crumbled fifty dollar bills into his hand, "Give these ladies two fifties." Taking what was left of Jahborn's blunt, A.W. said, "Come wait for me in the hallway," he told the women and then disappeared into the elevator.

Several minutes later both men were sitting in Jahborn's car. A.W was in charge of their Staten Island and Brooklyn operation when Jahborn was not around. A.W. had just finished updating him on the happenings since he'd been gone. "Word man," A.W. said, "And I think them motherfucking Jamaicans are at it again, but other than that, like I said, shit is still flowing. You know them niggas can't fuck with us," he boasted while searching through a stack of CDs for the Lox disc.

"So what you holding?"

"I got about twenty-eight grams left," A.W. said, "And Gizmo got all the money."

"Cool. So where Giz at now?"

"He should be at his castle. You want me to bring the car?" A.W. said referring to the new BMW they were parked beside.

"Naw, leave it there. How much dough Giz got?"

"About five gees."

"Umm, let's go get Giz," Jahborn said as their car veered down the street.

Smiling, A.W. said, "I miss your ass. So what's up my nigga—how was the trip?"

"That shit was the bomb son," Jahborn said checking his rearview mirror as the car breezed through the streets, "Let's pick up Giz and then I'll tell you both what the deal is, but first pass that blunt," Jahborn taunted him with a smile. Several minutes later he made a right turn down Sobel Court and pulled up alongside a dark brown building on Bowen Street. There, they both called up to a window, several seconds later Gizmo's head popped out; his voice echoing off the walls of the building across the street bounced down to them. In the next instant another head popped out of the window next to Gizmo's. It was his brother Snoop.

A.W. yelled up to them, "Yo, come down stairs yo!" Both men who were actually on their way outside anyway, disappeared from the window. A.W., climb through the car door window instead of opening it, sat back in his seat and puffed on the blunt, "Damn nigga how was the trip yo?"

"Chill son damn," Jahborn said coldly, "Wait for the rest of them niggas to get their asses down here so I won't have to repeat myself, aw'ight? Is that peace with you nigga?" He tried taking the chill from his voice. Smoke from his cigarette blew out of his nostrils. Before A.W. could respond to this the back door of the car opened and a tall, stocky, but flashy dresser name Gizmo slid across the seat making room for his brother Snoop who closed the door behind him.

"What's up my niggas?" Jahborn said to the men in the back seat.

"All that and all that." was how the back seat occupants replied before passing him a fat roll of money. "When you get back?" asked Gizmo.

"Today, baby," Jahborn said passing a freshly rolled blunt to Snoop who then asked, "So how was the trip player?" Just then A.W. started laughing which prompted Snoop to ask him, "Feather up your butt, nigga? What's so fucking funny?"

"Man I been asking this nigga the same shit since we got up, and he's turning it into some kinda mystery," The men all then looked at Jahborn who then began to smile. Reaching into his jean shorts, he pulled seven thousand dollars from each of the pockets, "Man I made twenty-eight gees real quick, now how's that for an answer?" He said not waiting for a response. "I coulda came back sooner but I had to lay my gee down with the chick, plus she took me around showing me some other places." He held the money up now, flashing it, "now how's that for an upstate move?"

"Then it's a gold mine up there, huh," the men concluded. It was more of a statement than a question.

"Yo, Giz—drive?" Jahborn said reaching for the door handle. Although he was the best driver out of them all, he didn't have a driver's license. "You know how Po' po' be fucking with me, plus you got license," he said climbing in the back seat. Gizmo slid behind the wheel playing the role of the chauffeur, he asked, "Where we going Jah?"

"First, stop off at the lab so we can pick up a few fifty sacks of that Dro' and then take me to the crib so I can put this cheddar up," he said leaning back in his seat.

Two hours later, after having stopped at the weed spot, the four men were now in East New York in Brooklyn at Jahborn's secret resting place that only a chosen few knew about which were only those who were with him now. As he entered the twenty-four story building on Cozine Street, which at one time was a Co-op, turned projects, its appearance was still maintained. Jahborn felt good about himself and the success he'd been having. He wondered what his older brother Unique would have to say now if he knew how good he was doing on his own.

The four men entered the elevator in the lobby along with other people which made it a tight squeeze. Silence prevailed as the elevator ascended, stopping almost on every floor. Only when the elevator was free of strangers did Snoop break the silence, "Yo Jah, what we gone do about them Jamaicans out in Shaulin?"

"Man, the way this upstate thing is going I'm about ready to say fuck that building and block we got out there, as well as our shit out here. We may be making just strictly out of state moves."

"Naw, fuck that man," said A.W., "We worked too hard to get that building flowing the way it is today, not to mention all the fucking drama and shoot outs we had over our block out there in Medina. Naw, fuck that shit man, I say we keep it all, and still get upstate money." A.W. said as the men now walked down the corridor on the twenty-first floor. A terrace was located in the hallway which gave a beautiful scenic view, if one enjoyed looking at sights of the ghetto. "I love living up here," Jahborn said, not bothering to respond to A.W.'s comment, "I feel like I'm on top of the world from up here," he said moving away from the terrace. A few seconds later they stood in front of a door marked 2146. Jahborn fished in his pockets for the key when the door opened, there, standing in the threshold, holding a plastic garbage can in her hand, wearing an exceedingly long pink Tee-shirt and pink fluffy bedroom slippers, stood Monica, Jahborn's girlfriend. She was light skin with perky, pretty pink lips, and long black hair. The sight of her hard nipples that poked against the Tee-shirt fabric, and lack of panty lining made it obvious to the men she was naked beneath the Tee-shirt. The Tee-shirt, long as a gown clung to her body, showing the outline of her figure as a gust of wind came from underneath the hallway door.

"Hi boo!" she said excitedly, after recovering from being startled by her man's presence. Dropping the trash can beside her she wrapped her arms around Jahborn's neck and gave him a long passionate kiss. After squeezing Jahborn's ass, as if seeing the other men for the first time she said, "What's up dogs?"

The men greeted Monica carefully, and made it their business not to stare too long, due to Jahborn's jealousy, and craze obsession over her which bordered on the brinks of lunacy. But from the looks of her exotic ass they couldn't much blame him. Monica continued to the incinerator with the garbage as the men entered the house. She called back to them as they entered, "Try not to make a lot of noise or slam the door y'all—I got a cake in the oven."

The men made their way through the apartment without replying but were careful not to let the door slam close. The apartment was filled with the aroma of all sorts of goodies being cooked, but the smell of cake mix dominated it all. Having smoked so much weed the four hoods were now starving and could think of nothing but ways to feed their munchies.

The apartment was a two bedroom duplex that had been left to Jahborn and his older brother Unique by their mother who since then had moved down south. Several years later Unique had moved out and left the apartment to Jahborn.

Jahborn had two kids of his own now, a boy and a girl by two different females; and no job other than his street employment—to which he was proud to have been doing so well in.

A.W., Gizmo, and Snoop made themselves comfortable downstairs as usual in the living room.

Having climbed the dozen or so steps leading to the bedrooms and bathroom, Jahborn now sat on his bed counting the money Gizmo had given him. Along with the money he'd made upstate, he separated the hundreds from the fifty's, from the twenty's and fives from the tens. Because he was serious about his counting and his back was to the door he hadn't heard Monica when she came in until she walked up behind him massaging his shoulders. Seductively she kissed him along the neck disturbing his concentration. It had been six long weeks since she last seen him, and to a person who was used to having sex every day, two to three times a day—that was a lifetime. She longed for his attention and affection. Turning his neck, Jahborn looked up into her face; Monica leaned down and kissed him knowingly and with signals. She then playfully pushed away from him, as a ritual, a prelude to the game. She closed their bedroom door, cutting off the rest of the world. She didn't care who was in the next room, nor did she complain about his long absence. It was he who kept her ass tight up in Luis and Versace and any other designer clothes she desired. Rewards rendered for his sporadic, yet torturing absence, she surmised. She knew that he knew that this was her time and that she planned to take relentless advantage of it. Walking seductively back towards the bed she reached down and pulled her Tee-shirt over her head, tossing it to the floor, and then stood still letting him feast upon the sights—a reminder of what he'd been missing. Her breast were full and round and without a sag. Her rib cage stood out against her skin, her smooth flat belly alluded to the fact that she didn't have any kids. Her curvaceous wide hips and mouth watering thighs acted as building blocks surrounding her well manicured rosebush, assured her long ago that anyone sampling her merchandise would be hooked for life. Despite the years he had been with her, Jahborn was always taken in by her striking beauty which left him breathless, stupefied, and sometimes speechless. Each time he seen her naked, like this, he wondered what possessed him to ever leave her side, for even a minute. Secretly, he feared that he would one day lose her, and therefore tried separately to get her pregnant so that this way if they ever parted ways he would always have an excuse to see her, and that they would have something forever connecting them together. Monica hovered over him, when her full, soft lips embraced his, her hand snaked down into his shorts caressing his manhood which felt like it had a fever in her hand. Without removing her tongue from his mouth she made him stand up, when his shorts dropped to his knees she used her foot to pull them down to the floor. Their tongues fought against each other as Jahborn's hands cupped her asscheeks, spreading them apart as though he was playing a cardigan. His hands then caressed her inner thighs and cupped her wet rosebush. Her pearl tongue juices, matting her hair, liquefied his fingers, making them sticky. They both were breathing hard now from the heated excitement. Jahborn, panting, wanted nothing more at the moment than to be inside her—deep inside of her. Breaking away from her he began throwing and spreading the money all over the bed making a sheet of it. It would be the most expensive sheet she'd ever laid on. When she grabbed his hand, stopping him, he looked at her—she pushed him down on the bed instead, laying him flat on his back. The horny look in his bloodshot eyes told her all she needed to know. He was like putty in her hands now, she was in total control. Their eyes held in a lock as she took one giant stride, stepping on top of the bed, and then lowered herself down onto him, and when he entered her, it felt like heaven.

Sometime later, spent and finally relieved of her restrained passion, Monica lay in Jahborn's arms. "Jah, the other day when I was coming in the building, that guy Cory and his friends that be standing in front of the building wouldn't let me through—and he was acting like he was gonna grab my ass when I pushed them outta the way." Jahborn knew the guy she was referring to name Cory; he lived in the building facing theirs. A small time drug dealer who had moved in the area within the last few years. What Monica neglected to mention was that there also was a guy with her who she'd met at the mall who had followed her home. She liked him and was actually considering sneaking off to a hotel with him in the future on one of those lonely, late dark nights' where she knew Jahborn would not be coming home . . .

Mentally, Jahborn envision Cory's smiling face as he caresses Monica's soft ass, and it caused his stomach to knot up. He grunted, "Word? Aw'ight, don't stress it, I'll take care of it, it's done and done." With her back to him now Monica smiled, satisfied that that base was covered. Suddenly she stood up, wrapped herself in a large beach towel and went to the bathroom to shower and dress so she could prepare dinner for Jahborn. Though the sex had been very satisfying it made him tired and lazy, he didn't feel like doing very much, however exhausted, his body stretched on the bed, and then he rolled out and up into a sitting position. The digital clock on the night table read 6:45. Time sure flies when you're having fun, he mused. Picking up his Tommy Hilfiger shorts he took out his Newport's, lit one and then made his way to the bathroom to wash up.

Making his way back downstairs in the living room where he'd left his partners, Jahborn heard Monica in the kitchen rambling through the draws. Snoop, stretched out on the couch was fast asleep while A.W. and Gizmo, smoking another blunt, entertained themselves playing video games. "Pass that blunt nigga," Jahborn said to Gizmo as he made his way between them on the couch in the sunken living room. He then called over his shoulder, "Yo Boo, bring something cold to drink."

"Okay," Monica called back, "dinner will be ready in a minute." True to form, seconds later she walked into the room carrying a long tray filled with four plates of steak, potatoes, cream corn, a large slice of cake and a pitcher of cherry Kool-Aid. Snoop was woken from his sleep and the four men wolfed down their food like they hadn't eaten in years, constantly complimenting the chef who only just smiled.

Twenty minutes later the meals were gone and the next blunt was lit by Jahborn, who asked, "Any of y'all holding heat?"

All three men raised their hands.

"Good, cause when we leave here we're going into the next building to pay this cat a visit and straighten something out before we head over to Newlots."

CHAPTER SIX

The proprietor of Club Velvet was one happy man; despite at times he worried about the success of his business due to all of his surrounding competition. Because his club did not fall from the lips of everyone's mouth in the glow of popularity, he knew that a great deal of its success was due to the location, which was right around the corner from another club called the Tunnel. A hot spot, popping and always jumping. Because of this sort of atmosphere the club Tunnel reserved the right in deciding who could come inside and who could not. Because the club's line sometimes lead into the next block the admission fee was sometimes also jacked up to at least a hundred dollars.

This, ironically, was a blessing in disguise for Club Velvet as more and more people who had been turned down at the Tunnel found their way to the doors of Club Velvet. Subsequently, this was not the case for both Unique and Infinite, who for tonight was maintaining a low profile due to the company that were with them.

Their male intuition warned them that if they went to the Tunnel club, their female popularity there would surely cause havoc and raised the hairs of curiosity of their monogamous companions. But even at Club Velvet tonight the men couldn't help but notice how unusually crowded and packed the club was with wall to wall women. Although a booty call was not in their program or the cause for them being there tonight, they took advantage of admiring all the cuties leaning against walls, standing at the bar, and sitting and chatting at surrounding tables.

The lights were dim yet did not prevent anyone from seeing what they wanted to see. Some of the patrons thought that the club's DJ had something against hip-hop since all he played was Reggae and contemporary R&B, but no one complained out loud. In fact, Trisha and her girlfriend Asia were having a lovely time, enjoying all the attention they were getting at the back of the club. Trisha had told her friend that she'd almost forgotten what it felt like.

As Unique, at the front of the club, busied himself talking with his friend Infinite, whom she considered psycho, she flirted back and forth with the seemingly endless line of men who had made it known that they were interested and available. But Trisha was no fool so she knew how far to go. In fact, she knew that whatever business her man was discussing at the front of the club had to be serious since he hadn't glanced her way once. If he had there was a good chance he would have seen the men who had given her their phone numbers since she declined to give them hers.

Trisha was not upset with Unique, and had no reason to be especially since he had kept his word in taking her out. He had even topped it off by having danced with her and only her for most of the night. And though she had her own money he had bought all of her drinks. She felt what more could a woman who'd been with a man for ten years could ask for. She sensed, however, that all of his niceties tonight were a meager attempt at getting her out of his hair. She also sensed that he seemed tensed, preoccupied, though he covered it well, she knew something was bothering him. However, long ago she learned not to pry.

Unique, sitting at a table with one leg crossed over the other with a glass of Hennessey in his hand focused in on Infinite, who, sitting across from him, stared into his glass of Thug Passion; a drink which had been tagged by the late rap artist Tupac Shakur, which consisted of part Remy Martin, part Alize` and part Crystol—guaranteed to get a dick hard and a pussy wet.

Unique leaned forward at the table, "So what the fuck's up. Is that all you got to tell me?" He barked at Infinite, he didn't mean to but he was upset with the way things had been going down with their business. When Infinite looked up from his glass Unique said, "Did you give that greedy ass cop Pataki his money?"

"Yeah," Infinite said, not liking the way Unique had been acting towards him, but understood that the last few turn of events had unnerved his homie. "I even let him pick the drop off place; the motherfucker had me meet him at some swingers club on 23rd. He said he can't stop the investigation and t—"

"Man," Unique said cutting him off, "Did you tell that fucking cracker we can't make no dough with all them cops crawling around the spot, its slowing down our cash flow?"

"Yeah, I told him man," Infinite said a bit irritant as he recalled his encounter with the cop. He didn't like the fact that he had been stuck with the task of having to deal with the cop either, but knew it was the price he had to pay as he paved his way on the yellow brick road to fame. Only if he had it his way, the cop would have had a fatal accident long ago.

"The motherfucker even made me pay for all his drinks, and said on the next drop off, for you to have your ass there. Man he was popping a whole bunch of shit."

Unique didn't like the cop either simply because he was a cop, but also because he was the cop who used the word "nigga" too much and so frequent that it made it easy to see he was a racist. "You gave him Blackseed's government name?"

"Yeah, but I don't think the motherfucker's gonna make an arrest cause all he kept saying was—what's the matter? Can't you—we, handle our own business?" And then the cracker had the nerve to say he didn't like snitches, man I wanted to shoot the devil, word God!" Both men had obtained Blackseed's given name and had forwarded it to the cop on their payroll to make an arrest for Chico's homicide. With it done this way it would be one less body count to come back to haunt them. They knew that they had plenty of skeletons in their closets because a lot of people had come up missing. And this is why on occasions both men had informed all of their workers of what would happen if any of them got arrested and decided to make a deal with the D.A. in exchange for their freedom. And though both men had preached this to their followers as though it was the gospel truth, secretly they both knew snitching was an intricate part of the game especially when it came to eliminating one's rival and competition.

As far back as the first time the men had met the cop Pataki, they could sense he was a loose cannon, and had a drinking problem which often revealed glimpses that he was also suicidal. Through later months of meetings and drinking with him they learned he was married and felt sorry for his wife as they realize he was a sadist and probably was abusive to his wife and kid.

Their initial arrangement with the crooked cop had been established when one of their worker's got caught by him during a drug sale. They cursed the day. It had been during the time when they were hustling out on the streets, because they had not been under investigation or anything they labeled the bust a humbug in that the cop just happened to be driving by when he spotted the sale going down. Because the cops had been by themselves, daringly, they boldly approached him with a proposition. It just so happened that they knew about a boosting ring of girls who went out in crews, taxing all the malls. And in exchange for their worker's freedom they gave the cop the name of a top flight booster who went by the name of Ignat, as well as the time and location of the store she was due to target. Thinking it was a trick which had often been plowed by dealers, the cop made his partner Giuliani hold their worker while Unique and Infinite went with him to prove their claim. Sure enough when they got to the store Pataki found Ignat, had even caught her in the act. After questioning and learning she had never been arrested before he gave her an ultimatum; 'Either fuck me and become mine or I'm locking your black ass up!' Knowing nothing about jail, fearing Riker's Island, Ignat agreed to sleep with the cop and shortly after became his mistress.

Draining the Hennessey from its container Unique slammed the glass down on the table as he leaned more forward, "What I wonna know is how the fuck y'all fail some simple shit like smoking a nigga? Some shit so easy that even my little brother could do if he was here," Unique said, making his point on how simple the task was.

Infinite, getting heated now himself which showed from the little hops he kept taking up and down in his chair as he spoke, "Man I told you the nigga wasn't out there, we had the whole block covered, we did the best we could—even wet motherfuckers up on G.P. just for knowing the nigga. Here, hold that down we told them, tell Blackseed it was for him. What more you want? What the fuck you expect? You want me to put a bounty on the nigga head?"

"Naw, I want the nigga dead, but I see that in order for that to happen I gotta do it myself. So just find out what hole the rat's in and I'll take it from there."

"What there? What? You think I'm a lame? Nigga I ain't no lame in this game, I know it's my job to take care of shit like this and I will . . . I know what needs to be done," Infinite huffed, looking at Unique. Looking back at him Unique said, "Then enough said, what's next on the agenda?"

"We covered everything."

"In that case, where's our women," Unique turned in his seat looking for Trisha.

"Both of them bitches is in the back of the club," Infinite said. "But yo, check out this pretty fucking picture over there."

"What? . . . Where?" Unique said following Infinite's stare until his eyes fell upon two voluptuous looking women at the bar, smiling, and looking at them. "Uumm," grunted Unique, "I see."

"I don't know if their brother's name is Keith, but they're definitely sweatin` us God." In tune with his partner's thoughts Unique raised his hand and flagged down a waiter. When the waiter approached their table he gave him fifty dollars and said, "Give those two ladies right there a drink. As many as they can get from this." As the waiter left he added, "Yo God, you ever notice the strange shit how whenever we're in these spots by ourselves, the bitches be acting all fishy and choosy. But as soon as you're already with your girl, bitches be giving you all types of signals and rhythm like they want to get with you?" Infinite began to laugh because what Unique was saying was true, he'd noticed it too.

"Well the trick to that is in finding a way of not letting them get by you whether you're with your girl or not," Capped Infinite with the belief that the club was big enough for them to make a pass at some other women without getting caught.

"Man, I ain't trying to hear Trisha's mouth tonight."

"I can dig it, but I always say what they don't know, won't hurt."

"In that case, I'm feeling you God, I'm feeling you." In tune to each other's thoughts the men rose at the same time from their table intending to join the women at the bar who at the moment were enjoying their free drinks, when suddenly both men were bumped from behind. "And just where the hell y'all think y'all going?" The man turned around, though they didn't have to, to know who it was, and looked into their women faces. Sitting back down Unique said to Trisha, "Good, I was just coming to look for you, now I don't have too."

CHAPTER SEVEN

They were all in attendance at the Masonic Temple Hall in Brooklyn; Junior Washington, his wife Karla, his daughter Kim, and his brother Daryle; brushing elbows amongst both local and distant politicians, community leaders, Reverends, Deacons, Borough Presidents and a few local celebrities—all the people who had once grew up in the neighborhood before they made it big and moved on to other areas. The event this evening was a fundraiser for the Aids virus research. Because Junior Washington and his family had been big contributors at other such functions they had been nominated to be a part of the welcoming committee tonight, greeting people as they came through the doors. Junior and his family had also helped in soliciting blocks of votes, at one time or another, for several of the politicians who were in attendance.

Ladies dressed in all white dresses, Eastern Stars; were in full charge of the food that was served at five hundred dollars a plate. Little girls dressed as they would look during the Easter Holiday, placed program fliers at each table. This Masonic Temple which had been transformed into a huge ballroom, with its high ceiling, was designed to hold up to four hundred people, found its occupants in somewhat of a tight squeeze. It was a Black Tie affair, and the two Washington brothers looked every bit the regal part; as splendid did the women in their gowns.

Subsequently though, the two youngest members of his family felt out of place. The new shoes Daryle had on were hurting his feet, and Kim felt restricted in her gown, wishing she could come out of it and into a pair of baggy jeans. Nevertheless, they were both happy that the next fundraiser in the months to come, to which they would be coordinating, would be a fashion show, and would enable them to dress down instead of up.

The night before last Junior had thought long and hard about the life he had been leading as a vigilante, and had come to the conclusion that he was hanging up his gloves in the war he single handedly waged against thuggish drug dealers, once he confronted the people whose name Blade Diamond had provided him with. He was closing the book on vengeance and moving on with his life.

He was no fool, which had allowed him to stay ahead of the game as he so far managed to escape all that he'd sowed, with a minimum of scrapes and bruises. He also knew things were not promised to remain that way. In fact, the laws of average said he was in line for a snag, having gotten away for as long as he had. Yet somehow, he had even managed to beat those odds, and was now right up there with those who were considered phenomenal. In his contemplation he'd also decided it was time that he bought a house for him and his family to live in. Something he could afford long before now, what with all the money he had expropriated from those while he was out on what he called his hunting spree. But he had been reluctant before now to buy a house because of the investigation he himself had done on suburban and rural areas where the landscape was eroding. Or the soil was semi contaminated due to toxic and chemical spillage, done accidentally, or on purpose by big industrial plants and companies whose millions of dollars, reaching the right hands, provided them the cover ups and white wash needed to keep a lid on from the public. Hush money, he called it. Yet two out of every five house wives who lived in these types of areas were diagnosed in the later years as having cancer or some other unexplainable illness which caused birth defects. Another reason Junior had been reluctant in buying a house was because he was a city person, and did not want to be like other people from the suburbs who had to commute each day from the suburb to work in the city, and then drive back only to have to do the same thing again tomorrow.

Yesterday Junior had grabbed a One Step camera from the closet, jumped in his jeep and rode around the areas just on the outskirts of the city limits, and took pictures of all the houses with for sale signs on them. He was now sitting at their table showing his family the pictures, discussing and getting their opinion on which house they should become the new owner's of. There were twenty pictures in all of houses and none under the price of five hundred thousand dollars. With money not being an issue, everybody at the table had picked a picture with the exception of Junior. His daughter Kim was the first to speak up, "I like this one daddy, the colonial house, plus it has a lot of extra acres."

"And I like this one," Daryle said pointing, "It's called the Manor. It's got a swimming pool in the backyard plus its only one hour's ride away from the city.

"Well, they're all basically an hour's ride from the city," Karla said, "Anyway, I like this one. And if it's safe to assume that Junior took all these pictures around the same area, then this brick house is the only one around that area like that—all the other houses are made of wood," pausing, Karla then said, "But wait a minute—you didn't pick a picture honey, which one do you like?"

"All of them," he said feeling caught. In truth, he didn't care. The house was really for them because he thought having one would make them happy. What he hadn't considered however, but now realized was that no two people in his family were alike and therefore had different taste and styles. Once he could get them all to agree on one of the house's he would then began his investigation on it, which meant amongst other things, finding out what industries were in the area, and checking the local hospitals to ascertain the ratio of its cancer patients and birth defects.

Several minutes later, as Karla and Junior engaged themselves in a side-bar conversation, they both observed Daryle and Kim when they went into a huddle themselves. Knowing how secretive and close the two were they had expected it sooner. They also were aware that the two younger family members were bored and clearly had made it known not long ago. So they were not the least bit surprised that no sooner than the motivational speaker Lester took the podium, that they heard Daryle announce,

"Yo June—Karla, I'm going outside for a few minutes to get some fresh air." Grabbing her sweater, Kim announced, "Me too . . . Wait for me Dee."

Both Karla and Junior watched as their daughter rushed to catch up with her uncle. Neither of them was fools and knew that Daryle and Kim were probably going outside to smoke weed to take the chill off their boredom. Having once been younger adults themselves, they remembered how the young suffered from the illusion that they, and only they, were the smartest people on the planet.

Junior knew that the most effective way to get the younger members of his family to keep things real with him was by not lecturing, dictating or being judgmental towards them. But when they did something that he strongly disapproved of he would take on the jargon that they used which he knew opened the passageway enabling them to see he could identify and relate to them as they would their friends and peers. Only after this was done would he apply the peer pressure. Experience had taught him that the youths were gullible, vulnerable and more susceptible to the pressures applied by peers than that of an adult or parent in their household.

"Damn, I thought I'd never get outta there," Daryle sighed.

"Me either," Kim said standing next to him just outside of the building, "And I still can't believe you ain't got no weed."

"Word. I told you I smoked the last blunt I had right after lunch." "Well, there's gotta be a weed spot around here somewhere, let's just stop the first person we see and ask them," Kim laughed. Daryle gave her a look that said he thought she was crazy.

"What?" she asked.

"I don't trust no shit I don't know about cause I ain't trying to smoke no garbage," he said now walking towards his car, "I'm going where I know they got the good good!"

"But what about D—," Kim looked back at the door of the Temple.

"You can go back in if you want, I'll be right back and I'll buy you a few bags." Kim stood still as she contemplated this, but only for a second, "Wait up Dee, shit," she said rushing to catch up.

Close to a half hour later, Karla was smiling, sitting at the table, holding her man's hand, "If there's one thing anybody can say about ole Lester, it's he ain't short winded."

Junior laughed at this, "Yeah, he's never been lost for words. Even back in school. But the good thing about it is he's always made sense when he speaks."

As Lester, the motivational speaker made his exit from the podium the audience began to clap loudly. Rising from their seats Junior and Karla joined the others in the standing ovation. Before anyone could be re-seated they heard the DJ place he needle on the vinyl and then the slow tempo lyrics of, `Sit back relax your mind/ just let my love flow through you/cause all of this time my love is with you/and you'll never have to worry cause I wonna spend my life with you—I love you`. The song I love you, by Keith Washington and Shaunta` Moore, set the pace and the mood.

"May I have this dance with the most beautiful woman in this room?" Junior said sticking out his hand. Teasing, and putting on the airs of pretense Karla's hand touched her cleavage as she looked around the room before asking, "Who me?"

Smiling, Junior replied, "Yes, of course you. You're the only pearl on this black sand beach."

"Well, since you put it that way, I'd be delighted sir," she said gliding into the folds of Junior's long muscular arms. As she snuggled her head into his chest she felt familiar hands slide down and then rested against the border line leading to her buttocks.

A minute or two later into the record Junior whispered, "Those two potheads have been gone for quite a while just to be smoking a blunt, don't you think?" Hearing the concern in his voice she looked up into his face, "I guess you have a point, let's say we give them five more minutes and if they're not back by then I'll break out the handcuffs when we go get them and I can cuff them to their chairs," Karla joked not wanting anything to spoil this special moment.

Daryl's car steered down Bushwick Avenue as Kim in the passenger seat chattered on, "I still say we should of went back and told them. We've been gone a long time just to be getting some air, they might start worrying. And you know they're gonna come down stairs, and when they see we ain't there they're g—"

"I know, I know, chill—damn. We're almost there already, just a few more blocks," Daryle said as Bushwick Avenue turned into Pennsylvania Avenue.

"Come on, let's go," Junior said grabbing Karla by the hand. They were heading towards the door at the front of the room when a rather tall distinguish looking man with gray at his temple accosted them, "Leaving so soon?"

"Actually, we're not Senator Johnson,' Junior replied, "Just making sure that some younger family members hasn't."

The senator chuckled and nodded his head knowingly. "I've had that problem once or twice myself,' he said, understandingly, smiling at their backs as Junior and Karla made their way down a flight of stairs leading out of the building. Outside they both began looking in all directions but found no signs of Kim and Daryle.

"Maybe they stepped around the corner, you know—not wanting to be all out in the open where people could see them," Junior said as he and Karla descended another flight of steps in front of the building. Not finding them around the corner, nor the opposite corner as well Karla seen the wrinkles begin to line her husband's forehead and knew it meant he was running out of patience and was fighting to maintain it.

"Oh, I know—lets go check Daryl's car, I bet that's where they're at." Although he gave her a look which said it better be, out loud he said, "Yeah, you're probably right." They walked to where Junior's SUV was parked; Daryl's vehicle had been parked behind it. Only now the parking space was empty. Not liking the feeling of this Junior said "That's it," and pulled a cellular phone from inside his jacket pocket. He beeped his brother. Karla stood in front of him hugging herself as they waited for the return call.

*　　*　　*

Just as Daryl's car neared the corner of Newlots his pager beeped. Snatching it from his hip he looked at the screen while he drove, "Ah damn!" He turned the corner and then stopped when he seen a public telephone.

"My father right?"

"Yeah," Daryle grunted, getting out of the car running to the phone. He picked up the receiver, place it to his ear only to find there was no dial tone. Looking at the phone closely now he saw that some demonic person, using firecrackers had blown the phone to smithereens. He quickly looked around him for another phone but found none.

"What happened?" Kim asked as he climbed back into the car. "The shit's broke and I don't see any more phones around here," he said pulling off.

"There's one right there," Kim said as they neared the next corner. Seeing the phone she was talking about in the middle of the next block he turned into, all the while observing the female who was using it at the moment. Her back was to him, but from what he saw she looked good. Pulling the car over he jumped out and walked over to the phone booth with the intentions of killing two birds with one stone. The tight black pants the female had on showing off her goddess figure caused Daryle to bite down on his finger inflicting himself with self-pain. He then said out loud, "Damn angel, I bet you're talking to God right now asking him to give you an extension on your stay with us down here on earth, but ah, Uumm . . . are you gonna be long?"

When Monica turned around to face him wearing a smile because of the compliment, Daryl's heart did a backward flip in his chest, and he barely heard her when she said, "Ten minutes."

"Ah, that's cold, you see, I really need to touch that phone there, but in the meantime I'll just fall back and enjoy the view." Stepping a few yards away he leaned against the fender of his car without taking his eyes off Monica's ass, despite Kim, who was leaning out the window at the moment chattering in his ear. Daryle was once the owner of a cellular phone until he learned he had to pay for both his outgoing and incoming call, to which he seen as the

State-of-the-Art robbery of the late 90's. But now that they had prepaid phones he was reconsidering buying one.

*   *   *

Monica was talking to Justice now, the guy she had met at the mall almost two months ago. They had gotten together a few times since then but as yet had not consummated their secret love affair through the conventional act of sex. Which was the subject they were discussing now. She liked him a lot because he had told her things she'd never heard before, and emotionally she felt like she was being pulled in opposite directions right now. He had just given her the ultimatum to either put up or he was pushing off. Having also just heard the comment that had been made to her by some guy, he used it against her, and anything else that would weaken her resistance to have sex with him.

"Don't do that to me Justice. I don't even know him," Monica said now raising her voice almost on the brink of tears. She ranted on. After a time of this when Daryle realized through her conversation that she had no intentions of getting off the phone any time soon, he was tempted to jump back in his car and search for another phone. But just at this conception his pager beeped again. Looking at the screen, following his brother's phone number was the code: 911 . . . 911 . . . 911. Getting pissed now Daryle walked back over to the phone just as Monica was putting another quarter into the phone slot. "Yo, what's up boo? You said you was only gonna be on there for ten minutes," he said watching her put yet another quarter into the slot, "But it's now twenty minutes later and you're still feeding money into the phone—what's the deal yo?" Spinning around to face him this time Monica rolled her eyes at him, and then gave him her back again as she continued her conversation. "I told you that I want to Justice, I swear I do, but I can't leave right now. I'm not lying. He brought me here with him, and he's right up the block in one of his spot's. Please don't do this to me Justice. Huh? . . . Yes, I love you." Hearing this only added to Daryle annoyance due to his urgency to use the phone. In this present state of mind he felt that

64

only a sucker would be standing and waiting like he was. Just then his pager beeped again, looking down he seen it was Junior.

Damn, this bitch just dissed` me. She must think she's all that. I shouldn't of been so nice—let me check this bitch, he told himself. He then banged hard against the phone booth, "Yo! What the fuck's up? I told you I have an emergency and need to use the phone!" Monica spanned around again, this time with venom, "Go find another phone! Leave me the fuck alone!" She said with tears now building in the corner of her eyes.

"Fuck that! Get the fuck off the phone!" Daryle barked slamming the lever down disconnecting her call.

"Okay motherfucker, now you done did it, now I'm going to get my man and he's going to come back and KICK YOUR FUCKING ASS!" She yelled from the top of her lungs, stomping out of the phone booth with tears rolling down her face.

"You piss color bitch! Go get your man. I should slap the shit outchu right now for dissing me," Daryle said picking up the phone receiver now dangling from its wire as Monica took quick steps down the block. He saw her entering a building as he began punching his brother's number into the phone. As the phone began to ring on the other end he looked over at Kim in the car, who gave him a-you're-evil-grin. He then jerked his head in the direction the female had took off, as if saying, `I don't know who the fuck she thinks' she is. When Kim seen Daryle taking a deep breath she turned in her seat as though it would prevent her from having to encounter the lashes Daryle was about to get from her father. He had a way of making a person feel stupid. Not finding the CD she wanted she proceeded to look in the glove compartment.

"I know, word, I know, and I'm sorry man damn. We were just on our way back now until you paged me and I stopped to call you back . . . Yeah, alright man, right now." Just as Daryle hung up and turned around he looked into Monica's face, she was back now with four guys who looked to be a few years younger than himself. He seen they were trying to look hard. As he was about to step out of the booth the four guys pulled their gats out on him.

"Yo, hold up son, what's the problem?" Daryle said trying to get free of the circle they were forming but two of the guys blocked his path.

"You like dis'ing females huh?" Jahborn said walking towards him now. He was itching to hurt someone since he hadn't as yet caught up with the guy Cory who also had dissed Monica. He was determined not to let this guy get away, this infraction couldn't ride.

"Naw, I didn't dis her man. I told her I had an emergency and needed to use the phone . . . to use the phone," Daryle repeated, almost tripping as he tried to back away from the guy approaching him with the gat in his hand, "And she told me she was only gonna be on there for ten minutes, but then she got into an argument with her man and stayed on there for another twenty minutes."

"What man nigga? I'm her fucking man."

"He's a liar daddy, I was on the phone with my girlfriend when he came over here and told me to get the fuck off the phone, and then hit me!"

"Yo, that's a lie, I didn't touch her man, and you can ask my . . . . Ahhhhh! . . . . Oh god!" Daryle jumped and screamed, "Ahhhhh," when Jahborn slapped him across the face with his gun. Daryle had paused, and within that second the other three guys were on him too. In an attempt to weave off their blows he slipped to the ground, as if waiting on this the four youths pounced. Out gunned and out manned it became evident that he could not defend himself, Daryle began to holler and beg for his life as the guys beat him as if he robbed their mother. When he rose an arm to fend off a blow Jahborn seen the wooden face Rolex on his wrist.

"Yo, oh shit, he's got a Rolly yo!" Jahborn shouted.

Gizmo, A.W., and Snoop charged at the watch on Daryl's wrist at the same time like pit bulls on the attack.

Kim, out the car now, crying, and screaming, shouted, "GET OFF HIM! GET THE FUCK OF HIM!" But each time she tried to come to Daryl's aid on the ground, the guns, constantly waving, in the men hands forced her back to the car. When Gizmo, the closest to Daryle reached down for his watch, forgetting for a second that he was scared, Daryle punched him in the face. Grabbing his mouth now, more embarrassed by the blow than anything else, Gizmo staggered backward. Moving in again now, this time enraged, he pushed Jahborn, A.W. and Snoop out of the way and began shooting Daryle on the ground. At the sight of this Kim began to scream hysterically from the top of her lungs as she watched in horror, Daryle begging god to make the guy stop shooting him. Monica stood froze still as Gizmo walked around the guy shooting him in the lower and then upper parts of his body. Kim watched on in utter disbelief, when it seemed as if the sight of blood made the other guys catch fever and joined in on shooting Daryle too. None of it seemed real. Just then they looked in Kim's direction, the looks on their crazed face frighten her even more as she realized she could be next. Feeling like someone had to get away, she had to get away to tell someone, to get help for Daryle. Screaming she jumped behind the wheel of the SUV whose motor was still running. Her hands shook uncontrollable as she gripped the steering wheel. Two years ago her parents had tried to teach her to drive. She had done well only in isolated areas, but once out in major traffic she became intimidated by passing cars, and had never drove any of the family cars. But an even greater fear gripped Kim now, as the unmistakable whiz of a bullet from one of the men's guns shattered the side back window. Throwing the shift gear into drive Kim's foot slammed down on the gas pedal as a cascade of bullets that followed, making thumping sounds, penetrating through the car, into the passenger seat, miraculously had missed her.

Forty blocks later Kim's vision was blurred by the tears gushing from her eyes.

Junior was walking in circles in front of the Masonic Temple as Karla tried to grab his hand to make him stop. She knew he was fuming and couldn't very much blame him. It was one thing to go outside and smoke a blunt, but to have just left without having told them first was something totally different. Now, topping that off, when he'd spoken to Daryle he had told them he and Kim were on their way back, but that had been almost an hour ago.

Junior only stopped pacing when he seen Daryl's car racing up the block towards them, swerving, and running the red light. Karla used this opportunity to squeeze Junior's hand. Their face went through several expressions of perplexities upon seeing Kim, jumping out of Daryl's car in the middle of the street where she left it blocking traffic. Seeing her parents Kim charged towards them. Upon the sight of her, the omission of Daryl's presence, and her erratic behavior, Junior knew immediately that something terribly wrong had happened. Kim ran straight into her father's arm screaming, ranting, "THEY KILLED HIM DADDY, THEY KILLED UNCLE DARYLE! THEY KILLED UNLE DARYLE . . . THEY KILLED HIM . . . THEY KILLED HIM!"

"Who . . . where? Junior shouted trying to force her face away from his chest. She was shaking uncontrollable against him. "Who I said? Where?"

"They just kept shooting him . . . They just kept shooting him . . . Shooting him and Shooting him and Shooting him!"

"Who? . . . Where, Godamit?"

"They killed him . . . They killed him . . . All of them . . . All of them killed him!" She sobbed even more now.

Knowing the trauma she had been through when she was younger, and seeing the traumatic state his daughter was in now, bought home the fact that the insidious clawing hands of death had once again reached out in the dark a struck his family a mighty blow. This fact frustrated him more causing a lump to swell in his throat. As he loosen his tie, car horns sounds caused him to turn and he see Daryl's car in the middle of the street, still blocking traffic. He looked at Karla, "I'm going to move the car. Try and get her to make some sense by the time I get back." Hugging her daughter to her Karla watched as Junior ran into the street dodging cars of impatient drivers who began riding around Daryl's car blocking their path. Parking the car Junior returned to his family who by this time were sitting on the steps in front of the Temple. Kim appeared a little calmer now and with her mother's help had told Junior the horror story of what had happened.

"Get up. Let's go."

"Where we're going?" Karla asked while helping Kim up by the shoulders.

"Kim's going to show me where my brother is," Junior said throwing his wife a set of keys, "Here take my truck, I'll follow y'all."

A half hour later, from a short distance away they could see the beacons from police cars flashing in the night just up ahead. The beat of Junior's heart accelerated and his palms became sweaty. He honked his horn indicating for Karla to stop, she did. Getting out of Daryl's SUV Junior walked over to the Karla's window. "Leave the vehicles here and we'll walk the rest of the way." Out of the car he clued them in on what and what not to do and say.

Arriving on the scene there were spectators everywhere. Police in uniform, plain clothes and suits. An ambulance van was on the sidewalk, a patty-wagon from Brookdale Hospital morgue was double parked on the street. Little kids were pushing each other out of their way so that they could get a better look. Two men with cameras in their hands were leaning over a body, snapping shots, on the ground, next to a public phone booth that was cordoned off with yellow tape. The sight of the tape caused Junior's heart to drop. As the unreality that it was his little brother laying on the ground, who according to his daughter, had been murdered in cold blood,

Made his blood boil. He wanted it to be a mistake, that she had made a mistake—that she didn't know what she was talking about—that she'd gotten hold to some powerful weed and had had a bad experience which caused her to become delusional. That it wasn't his brother laying on the ground but someone else's brother because his brother was somewhere else.

As they got closer Kim began to cry again and shaking. Junior stopped, turned around and held her by the shoulders, looking into her eyes he said, "Don't say nothing to the cops, you hear me? If any of them ask you a question you don't know nothing about nothing, all you know is that's your uncle and he's dead." Walking closer to the scene Kim became overwhelm by the pain and now confusion. She didn't understand why her father said what he just said. Wasn't it the police job to find and then lock up the people who did this?

So how could they do that if she couldn't tell them what she saw and what they looked like? Not wanting his daughter nor his wife getting involved more than they needed to, he walked a few feet ahead of them and was stopped by a cop in uniformed as he reached the cordoned off area. "What . . . Are you people blind or something? Clear the area, back up there guy," The cop said attempting to push Junior back but he suddenly realize he had run into a brick wall when his hand touched Junior's chest. Silently, the cop told himself he hoped he'd never have to run up on this guy on some dark street without back up. Looking at Junior and the two women who were just a few feet behind him, judging from the way they were dressed, he knew they were together and probably had something to do with the corpse on the ground since he too had on a suit identical to the man standing in front of him. Surmising that they could be related he figured he should perhaps change his attitude, "Can I help you guy?"

"I have reasons to believe," Junior nodded his head, "that that's my brother over there on the ground." The cop didn't like the feel he was getting from this guy. Having worked the streets for ten years he trusted his instincts. The guy's eyes were a dead giveaway; they were like looking into the eyes of a dead fish. The cop yelled over his shoulder, "Hey Mack—got some people over here who thinks the deceased is a relative."

A short white man in a suit with receding hair and a cigar in his mouth walked over. "Is that right? And what makes you think that?" He asked looking Junior's suit up and down but drawing the same conclusion as the uniform cop.

"He called me over an hour ago telling me he was right here and that he was on his way to join me and my family who at the time were at a fundraiser. Only when he didn't show we got worried and decided to come and see for ourselves what was holding him up."

Although it was a very hot and humid night the homicide detective suddenly realize that since standing next to this guy he felt a cool chill equivalent to someone opening a freezer door inside an otherwise warm room. Shrugging it off, the detective said, "Come with me."

Bending underneath the rope Junior followed him. When the detective noticed the two women following behind the man he stopped and said, "You sure you want them to see this?" Junior looked at Karla and Kim, turned back around to face the cop and said, "Death is a backward reflection of life. If we can bear the gruesome realities of life, we should also be able to do the same when it comes to death," he intoned in an even voice.

The detective raised a quizzical eyebrow as he stared at Junior. Just then Karla whispered into Kim's ear, "You don't need to see him again, stay here." She then followed the men as they stood in front of a body on the ground. When she looked down and seen that it was really Daryle laying in a puddle of his own blood with one of his arms twisted behind and underneath him, her stomach turned over and she felt like she wanted to regurgitate, forcing the bile back down, Karla braced herself.

"Is this him?" The detective asked.

"Yeah . . . it's him," Junior replied taking a deep breath.

Crying, Karla shook her head up and down.

"Well, it looks like it was a robbery that went sour," the detective said, "There's signs to indicate he resisted his attacker or attackers. There's no wallet or money in his pockets and the marks on his wrist indicates he was wearing a watch but now it's gone. Was he wearing a watch or have one on when you last seen him?"

"Yes, a wooded face Rolex," Junior intoned, remembering he had gotten it for Daryle for his birthday. Junior took off his suit jacket and placed it over his little brother's body. Twenty questions and a half hour later Junior, and Karla walked back to where they had left their daughter standing. The closer they got, from the look on Kim's face Junior could tell something else was wrong. Not letting on he waited until they were a few yards away before looking into his daughter's frighten face. "What's wrong Lady?"

"Them, she whispered, "I think I seen one of them who killed uncle Daryle."

"Where?" Realizing his mistake almost too late, quickly he checked it, "No! Wait, don't point, just stand right here in front of me and describe the person to me, what he look like." Junior knew in a lot of cases the culprit always came back to the scene of the crime, lots of times to find out how much cops knew, and also to learn who was talking, and in some cases just for the thrill of it.

"It's hard for me to describe him Daddy," Kim said staring into the crowd of spectators.

"Try!" Junior demanded.

"He keeps moving in and out behind people."

"Then describe what the person's wearing that he's standing next to." "That girl right there with the extensions in her hair, wearing the white shorts and the red tank top, he's standing next to her . . . . right behind her."

Junior's trained eyes trailed in on the person his daughter had just described, and in the next instant had seen the guy. He was using the body of the crowd as a shield of cover that yet allowed him to see what he wanted to. He was young looking. "I got him," Junior whispered. "Now I want y'all to get in the truck and go home."

"And what about you? What are you gonna do Junior?" Karla asked and then regretted it when the Ghetto Soldier spun around and coldly said, "I said go home." He then turned back around facing forward again making sure he didn't lose sight of his quarry.

"Come on mommy," Kim said pulling her mother's arm as she had an inclination of what her father was going to do, all that she didn't understand in him telling her to keep quiet now began to make sense. As if picking up on the same thoughts that her daughter was entertaining Karla hugged her daughter's shoulder and quietly walked away. She had suspected such things about her husband long ago, the way he was behaving now only confirmed it, and she shivered.

Jahborn lighting a Newport looked at the time on the new Rolex on his wrist and began talking to the girl standing next to him. The Ghetto Soldier took mental pictures of the young guy's face just as he smiled at the girl.

CHAPTER EIGHT

A.W., Gizmo and Snoop were riding in the Acura Legend which tagged closely behind Jahborn's Q-45 Infinity, which at this time were only a few cars ahead of them. Each man was looking forward to having some fun as a mean to relieving some of the pressures they faced daily and was feeling the crunch of lately.

It had been a week ago that they had armed themselves and had been watching and waiting but nothing had happened. Today was the eighth day since the threat. They had left the spot not too long ago still feeling that since they hadn't done anything in the face of the threat that had been made against them, that it had added a blemish to their reputation as being `murder one niggas`. Word had already spread through the streets about what had happened, just as word had spread about the guy they bodied not too long ago. They had been happy about that because it would let people know that they weren't to be fucked with because they weren't playing no games. So they had been itching for the guys to come back around so they could make another example and add a few more notches to their belts.

It wasn't the first time people had tried them, and they knew as long as they were in the game it wouldn't be the last, there would be others—they always were. But they had no problem with that, however, just for today, they were looking forward to bagging some cuties, smoking some trees and winning some money, it was why they were in the area.

Unique and Infinite were in the front seat of his Lexus which cruised slowly down the streets of Harlem, while Flavor, Brice and Hot Tee, sitting comfortably in the back seat, rolled blunts.

Infinite, who could have bought a car long ago, had held off since he rode around with Unique in his Lexus practically everywhere—was stacking his money to buy a Land Cruiser. Everyone in the car today was high and happy. It was Unique who had suggested that they take today off from hustling and grinding and were now about to enjoy a fun filled afternoon watching a basketball game in Holcombe Rucker's park on 155th street and 8th avenue.

In the past many of them had won thousands of dollars by betting on the games played in this park. And it was with those same intentions which at the moment caused Unique to have a smile on his face as he turned on 8th avenue. As he expected he seen that the parking lot across the street was already filled with cars by those who had gotten there early to assure they would get good parking space as well as a good seat at the game. At the moment the men in the Lexus kept their eyes peeled for a place for them to park while feeling the sounds of, `Don't wonna be a player no more, I'm not a player I just crush a lot,` by Big Punisher and Joe, that was getting at them through the car's stereo speakers. Without warning, Brice shot forward in his seat which caused Hot Tee to spill the weed in his lap on to the carpet floor. "Shit! Brice!" Paying attention now Unique seen what he considered a rarity space when he dug a chick sitting behind the wheel of a 911 Porsche, pull out of her parking space and into traffic. Without a moment to waste he swerved towards the vacant space.

Having already drove pass it, Jahborn was not aware of the parking space he had missed until he looked into his rearview mirror and by this time it was too late, yet he had caught glimpse of the car A.W.'s was driving that almost collided with another car.

"Get that shit right there!... Right there son!" Gizmo had yelled, pointing to the vacant space that the girl in the white Porsche had pulled out of. Though they were on the opposite side of the street A.W. made a dash for the vacant space as if it was the passageway to eternal life, but another car had the same idea. A.W., thinking fast, slammed on the brakes to avoid hitting the Lexus that had cut in front of them and into the parking space. "What the fuck!" A.W. barked, slamming the gear into park. Heated, he, Gizmo, and Snoop jumped out of their car talking about the ass whipping they were going to put on the occupants in the Lexus whose tinted windows prevented them from seeing inside.

Unique, Infinite, Flavor, Brice and Hot Tee, unaware that the occupants in the other car had gotten out and coming their way, were laughing happily that they had gotten the parking space. They were also preoccupied with counting their money as they climbed out of their car, separating their gambling money from what they could not spend.

"Oh shit," Hot Tee said being the first to look up and seeing the vaguely familiar faces. "Ain't those them young cats that ran in the building on us in East New York that day?"

When the men looked up and into the faces of A.W., Gizmo and Snoop, A.W. shouted "Yo that's them same niggas who told us we had to shut down."

"Damn sure is, word up," Gizmo said, not believing his eyes, "Yo, we gonna ride down on them niggas for real now." Sticking his hand underneath his big jerseys, Snoop barked, "Remember us?"

"Yeah! What's up partner?" Spat Gizmo.

Unique, not all together clear on what the hell was going on since everything was happening so fast, nevertheless, replied, "Whatever you want to be partner," he spat back, "Y'all finger fucking y'all thug passion underneath them shirts like we suppose to be scared and shit, but as soon as y'all make some noise it'll draw the attention of the rest of my boys and I can guarantee none of you niggas will get off this block," he told them with confidence, "In fact you niggas . . . hold up—wait a minute," he suddenly said staring at A.W. "You look familiar nigga, I know you. You look like this little nigga who use to be with my little brother."

The more Unique talked, the more A.W. began to realize who was talking to him, as the realization sat in he breathed, "Oh shit. Word, you're Uiee, right?"

"Yeah nigga," Unique grinned, pulling him to him in an embrace, "Where the fuck is my brother at? You seen that nigga lately?"

"Yeah, he's with us now." No sooner than he said this Jahborn's car pulled up beside them with the window rolled down. "What the fuck's going on?" Jahborn said with a smirk, stunting now that he seen his brother. He pulled the car over, got out and started bee-bopping back towards them.

"Look at this nigga stunting, class is in session," Unique said smiling and then pulled his brother to him, hugging him. Watching the two brother embrace, Gizmo and Snoop sneaked their hands out from underneath their shirts and swallowed hard as they realized how close a call it had been. Everything had happened so fast Snoop hadn't as yet removed the frown from his face. Unique looked at his brother Jahborn a second time, jerked him by the neck to him again, "Why you been ducking me man?" He said remembering that his little brother had been avoiding him every since he had told him he couldn't get down with his crew. He had even went to the extreme measures of camping out in front of their mother's old apartment for Jahborn but still hadn't manage to catch him.

"I ain't been ducking you nigga I been busy," Jahborn said pulling away from him.

"A whole year, huh? Give me a break nigga! But anyway, forget that, we've found each other again and that's all that matters," Unique said wrapping his arm around Jahborn's shoulders. The men began to walk in the direction of the park at the corner across the street. Suddenly Jahborn stopped, turned around and threw his car keys to A.W. "Yo, park my shit son, try and find some place close by."

A.W. got into Jahborn's car as Snoop did the Acura, and together they looked for parking space as the rest of the men went into the park.

It was the second game and two hours later. Unique and Jahborn were sitting next to each other. Their voices were hoarse as a result of yelling their suggestions to the men on the court playing ball. Unique was up Seventy-five hundred dollars and happy. Jahborn was thirty-five hundred dollars in the hole for having bet on the team that lost. Looking to get back what he lost he now betted on the team Unique betted on who was now up by twelve points.

Upon their arrival, Unique and his crew had reserved seats in the front role. At one point Jahborn thought that there would be a problem since he and his crew did not. But Unique had whispered something into Infinite's ear who then walked off for a few minutes and when he returned he just nodded his head, and just that simply everything had been settled.

Unique, at the moment was boasting about he was seriously thinking about starting his own basketball team, and then spun around to Jahborn sitting next to him, "Yo my man Everlasting was telling me about y'all cats. Damn, when he said it was some crazy niggas I should have known it was you." He said pushing Jahborn lightly by the shoulder, "I'm sure glad he ain't do nothing to you cause then we would have had beef." The worker name Justice who Unique had intended to put in control of the spot before he found out it was his little brother's, had told him about a chick whose back he was digging out, had a man who hustled around there in East New York, and that he had killed a man for having disrespected her. He intended to ask Jahborn if he knew anything about it, just out of mild curiosity, since it was his brother's area, and he liked to stay abreast of all gun clappers. But he had gotten side tracked when a guy on the team he was betting on had missed an easy layup. He stood up in his seat to let the guy know just how dumb he thought that was. As time moved on they had moved on to other topics and it had slipped Unique's mind. By the end of the second game, to which they also had won, they had discussed various issues and business problems and how they might be able to help each other out. Unique had told Jahborn about his trouble with Blackseed, and Jahborn had told him about his potential troubles.

CHAPTER NINE

Junior Washington had buried his one and only brother. The funeral had been a huge turn-out which proved he hadn't realized how well known and loved his brother had been. In retrospect, he thought how strange it was that Daryle had died only thirty blocks away from where he had been born. It left him to ponder if his little brother had ever paid any attention to his birth certificate. As if it was only yesterday he remembered climbing out of bed bright and early in the morning, walking through the snow to the bus stop where he had caught the number ten bus to Brookdale Hospital where he picked up his mother and his new born baby brother. The fact that they had different fathers meant nothing. He was content that he now had someone, a brother who could plunder and roam the streets with him when he became old enough. He had intended to teach him everything he knew. Only it hadn't turn out that way. This had been twenty-five years ago.

Junior had let Kim take over from where Daryle had left off in the production company knowing how close to the two of them were. She had spent just as many hours in that studio as Daryle did. Had even been grounded once or twice for it too. Knowing that she knew how to work and engineer the equipment, he decided to let her take over because he knew Daryle would like that. After Daryl's funeral he had been taken aback by Kim's suddenly persistent and abrupt questionings. Without asking him right out, she had asked in every other roundabout, conceivable way a daughter could ask a father to be part of something she wasn't even suppose to know existed, or let on that she knew or had suspicions about. Although he knew what she was hinting at, he played dumb and would not encourage her, yet secretly, his ego and pride, the side of him that regarded his genes stock, caused him to wonder just how she would fair if he was to take her out with him on what he called his hunting sprees.

Years ago he had taken Daryle out with him, since Daryle had been victimized by the drug game it would be the inspiration, the fire burning within that would enable him to strike out against an atrocity that had almost taken him down. But Junior had learned the hard way that motive alone was not good enough to horn the skills needed to become a practitioner in his trade. And subsequently, Daryl's lack of skill had almost gotten both of them killed when Daryle had allowed the knock at a door to distract his attention from a person, who under the present situation had nothing to lose.

Since the night Junior had found his little brother dead, he had done his homework by following the guy who returned to the scene after having participated in Daryl's killing. Trailing him, he learned all the vital information needed; who the guy was, his name, where he lived, how many women he had, and the people he hung out with. He had then followed them around and learned who they were and the people they hung out with. Before long he had folders on all of the main guys from the description his daughter gave plus more.

Intermittently, Junior Washington black BMW circled the block of Sheffield and Newlots until he was content. When the time was right he parked his car half a block away and walked back. From there the Ghetto Soldier crept into the small four story tenement building in the middle of the block. From what he could tell while making his way up the first flight of stairs, there appeared to be only four apartments on each floor. Nearing the second landing he wondered how these people who sold drugs in the building made money when the customers had to climb three flights of stairs to get it. But then realized that when it came to crack and its powers, a fiend would climb a ladder that extended to the moon to get it. Reaching the third floor, he suddenly heard laughter and then seen several people from the fourth floor descending the steps. It was one o'clock in the morning but he knew that people in the hood never slept. Slowing his pace he avoided eye contact as the people passed him by. Seconds later he cursed beneath his breath as he witnessed two more guys coming out of the apartment that he intended to enter. Avoiding eye contact with them as well, he quickly made his way up the next flight of steps, only instead of stopping on the fourth floor he made his way to the landing on the roof.

Pushing through the door he rushed to the front of the building and looked over the edge seeing the two men walking down the street and entered a green Honda Accord. He had noticed the car when he circled the block because he'd once own one of the same color, year and model. From the roof's ledge he watched the two men in the car drive off. He crept back into the building and down to the third floor. Placing an ear to the door he listened for movement before pulling out his gadgets and did a number on the lock on the door. As he worked he noticed the hole where the cylinder of another lock had been but had now been removed so that drugs and money could be pushed through. Sixty seconds later the lock sprung. Junior slid quietly into the apartment whose hallway lead directly into the living room. Removing a .45 from his waist he crept further into the room where he seen a man's body lying on a couch. A stack of money lay on the floor beside him. Next to the money was a medium size brown paper bag filled to the brim with crack vials. Although the man's eyes were closed the Ghetto Soldier didn't know if the man was merely resting his eyes or sleeping until he heard a light snoring coming from him. By passing the man on the couch he crept into the bedroom where he found another man, though fully dressed, lying across the bed sleep.

The roach of a blunt lay in the ashtray next to him, which told him the man, was sedated. He also noticed a chrome .357 with a black rubber grip handle within reach on the night table. Junior inched slowly towards the bed with his gun raised in the event the man suddenly woke up and reach. Picking up the .357 with a gloved hand he placed it in the center of his back, and then leaned over the sleeping man placing a hand over the sleeping man's mouth while pressing his .45 to the man's temple. Startled, the young man's eyes opened immediately, when he accessed the situation his eyes quickly shifted towards the night table for his gun noticing it was gone. He then looked back into the eyes of the man hovering over him who was shaking his head from side to side. Getting the message, Junior then witness the transformation of fear as it entered the man's eyes, he could see it now, and it was what he was waiting for. He leaned down even further now and whispered, "We're going into the living room where your man is at. I ain't gotta tell you what will happen if you try something cause you already understand, don't you?"

The young man jerked his head up and down understandingly before Junior released his mouth. Snatching him by the collar he led him into the living room. He had decided that since neither of these two men were a part of the main ones who had killed his brother he would spare their lives and leave them to deliver the message. But then instinctively he knew there was going to be trouble when he entered the living room and found that the man was no longer lying on the couch. His eyes searched the partially dark room and then seen him when he quickly looked to the left of him. The man had been standing by the windowsill with his back to them but turned back around and seen someone holding his friend. Shock registered on his face and he immediately reached for his waist.

"Don't do it!" Junior hissed strongly. But at this same time the guy he held captive tried to break free. Catching him by the arm Junior yanked him back to him. But the guy by the window at this time had fired two shots aimed at the Ghetto Soldier but hitting his friend instead. Junior squeezed off three rounds hitting the guy called Tank in the chest, but Tank, living up to his name, kept coming and shooting, hitting the corpse of his friend that Junior was using as a shield, while squeezing off two more shots that open up a hole the size of a mouth above Tank's mouth which caused him to stagger back and fall. Dropping the dead man he had still been holding in his arm, Junior cursed as he headed for the door disregarding both the drugs and money that were out in the open.

The act which just happened had now changed his thinking as he vowed that no one's life now would be spared.

*   *   *

Kim was sitting in the living room watching late night T.V. when Junior entered the house carrying his black bag. From the way she acted he'd gotten a feeling she had been up waiting for him. Upon seeing him, she jumped up and rushed towards him, "Hi Daddy!"

"Hey baby," he intoned, ". . . Something wrong?—where's your mother?" '

"No, nothing's wrong," she said before arching on her toes to kiss him, "And moms in her room sleep."

"Oh," he said checking himself, but with relief in his voice.

"Daddy," Kim said now looking him directly in the eyes, "Can I help you?"

"Help me what Boo Bear?" he asked staring back.

"With . . ." she hesitated, ". . . with your bag?" She said dropping her eyes. The silence between them grew pregnant as he received the feeling he had gotten before about her. She wasn't saying what she meant. He then broke the silence, "It's not that heavy baby, I can manage, but thanks anyway." He walked toward his room, stopped, turned around and asked, "Is everything alright at the studio?" Kim shook her head up and down still avoiding eye contact.

"Boo Bear," he called and only then did she look up. "You know you can talk to me about anything, don't you?" She shook her head up and down again. When a few seconds past and she still hadn't said anything, he said, "Night Boo Bear."

"G' night Daddy."

He entered his room.

*   *   *

It was early Sunday morning, a green Honda Accord was in the Brownsville shopping area of Brooklyn, cruising slowly down

82

the streets of the Flea Market on Belmont. Even at this early hour the stores on both sides of the streets were crowded with shoppers. The streets themselves were littered with debris and wooden boxes that was used by merchants who sold their merchandise on top of them outside of stores. This lucrative Oasis also created vehicle congestion.

Every so often the Honda Accord made pit stops and two young men jumped out making a dash into a store where they purchased fresh vegetables, foods and fruits. The car was now parked in front of a fish store. Several minutes later the men emerged carrying bags, climbed back into the car and the Honda pulled off from the curb. The car made a right turn on Mother Gaston, formerly known as Stone avenue and then a left turn at the corner of Sutter Avenue. None of the occupants in the car were aware of the man on the peddle bike which trailed fast behind them.

Because it was early morning these streets were scarcely occupied by walking pedestrians and those who were about paid no attention to the man dressed in black riding the ten speed bike a bit too small for him. Nor did anyone notice the lever on the bike which allowed it to be fold in half. When the Honda Accord stopped at a red light on the corner of Junius, Junior Washington rode up alongside the car's window on the driver's side. As soon as the young driver looked up and over at the guy on the bike his face exploded into fragments of meat as the bullets from the gun in the bike rider's hand, ripped into his flesh. The man in the front passenger seat screamed, before urinating on himself, using a bag of groceries as a shield as he scrambled to get away. He was trying to unlock the door when three bullets cutting through the bag ate into his face. The foot of the driver on the brake pedal, who was now slumped over the steering wheel, weakened which caused the car to run into another parked car.

Initially, when the roar of the loud gun shots broke through the silence of the morning, the people on the streets who knew about the notorious reputation of the neighborhood, did not stop to look or investigate, but ran the opposite direction from which they heard the gunfire.

Junior Washington, peddling fast on his bike, dismounted a few blocks away where he popped the trunk and folded the bike before putting it into the trunk of his car. Closing the trunk, he looked around him making sure he wasn't being watched. Climbing behind the wheel, his vehicle drove off.

CHAPTER TEN

It was now a week later and Jahborn was at his apartment in Brooklyn. As he came into the building a few guys standing out front told him that the guy Cory heard he had been looking for him, and that Cory was now looking for Jahborn. Before entering his building Jahborn, A.W., Gizmo and Snoop went to the guy Cory's house in the next building only to be told that Cory wasn't home. Jahborn then pushed the issue of Cory to the back of his head in as much that he now had more pressing matters to focus on.

Someone had hit his spot on Sheffield and Newlots. The most puzzling part about it was that no drugs or money had been taken. To him, it smelled like a hit, in fact, he knew it was. What made him so sure of this was that the very next morning two more of his workers had gotten rubbed out when their car had stopped at a red light in Brownsville. Because he didn't have a clue who had done it, he was at first baffled, shaken up, and then enraged with anger. He didn't like the feeling or the fact that someone now had him spooked since it was a condition he had often left others in.

Every young youth from the area who roamed the streets, who looked up to Jahborn and wanted to be down with his crew, had been promised a job and would be taken shopping with the crew if they could provide a name, a lead, anything that would put them in the know of who had hit his men. Normally where Jahborn and his crew's attitude toward other people was arrogant and insulting, suddenly now became docile and extra nice.

It was a crack head couple who had rented their apartment out to them, but when the cops had arrived on the scene investigating the double homicide, and the landlord caught the scene of his building on the news that involved murder, drugs, and money, he had evicted the crack head couple.

Jahborn had spoken to his brother last night about the dilemma and agreed to put their ears to the ground and get together a few days later once they had a handle on the situation. As it stood, Unique thought his man of, Everlasting sent someone to do it since Unique had forgotten to contact him in jail to let him know there'd been a change of plan since he learned that the shorties was his younger brother and his crew.

At the moment, Jahborn was leaning most of his body weight on the arm of the couch. This act itself was proof that his girl Monica was not at home, or she would have given him a lecture on how black people weren't use to having anything good cause if they did they wouldn't lean on it to tear it up. Around ten o'clock this morning she informed him that she was going shopping with her girlfriend who lived downstairs. Having no reason to doubt it he hadn't question her, plus since the way she had broken down during the last incident where they killed a guy in front of her, he didn't want her around hearing what they had been discussing since daybreak.

"Like I was saying," Gizmo said from the couch with his feet propped up on the coffee table, something else that would not have been done had Monica been home, "I think it's somebody we know real good, and they're trying to move in our shit son."

"Yeah, but who?" A.W. said sitting next to him. Snoop, sitting in a love seat across from them, stood up, sucked air in between his teeth, which indicated he was fed up, discussed or both, said, "Man, we been going over this same shit over and over again since last night and it ain't getting us nowhere. I say let's just pick a motherfucking herb; put some fire underneath his ass—I bet he'll start talking . . . This shit we're doing now ain't gone get us nowhere. I'm going to the corner store to get some more blunts . . . . anybody want something?" He said heading for the door.

"Yeah,' Gizmo yelled over his shoulder, "Bring me back a 40 of Old E."

Exactly a minute later Snoop emerged from the elevator on the first floor lobby and exits the building. The bright shining sun assaulted his eyes forcing him to put on his sunshades. Several minutes later he entered the store, "Let me get a pack of Newports and five Dutch masters," he said to the Puerto Rican man behind the counter. While the man reached into the box for the cigars he kept an eye on Snoop who looked like the type who would steal something as he continued to walk down the aisle to the freezers at the back of the store.

As if it had been time, to which it had been, a white, two doors, BMW pulled up in front of the store. Though there weren't many people out on the streets at this time, a casual glance from those who were, would have noticed that the car didn't have any license plates on it. And had anyone noticed, they didn't let on. Nor did anyone seemed to pay close attention to the statue of a man dressed in all white who emerged from the car and headed into the bodega with the car's engine still running.

The owner of the store was still behind the counter when he noticed the tall man entering his store pulling a white object down over his head that at first looked like a cap but actually was a ski mask. Whispering a silent prayer in Spanish, he raised his hands above his head as he backed away from the counter. He had been stuck up twice before within the last six months and knew the drill. Only now it appeared that the mask man was no longer paying him any attention, and he had proof of this as he just walked pass him and into the back of the store. At this exact time, Snoop was bending down, reaching into the freezer for a 40 ounce bottle of Old English 800 when he suddenly felt something or someone behind him. From the squatted forward position he was in, he turned around and looked up, it was at that moment he seen the gun and his brain froze of all coherent thoughts. Instinctively, or perhaps out of the fear of realizing there was nothing he could do, Snoop closed his eyes, but it did not stop his ears from ringing the loud noise explode from the gun. He felt the heat on his face and even seen the bright spark of light behind his closed eyelids. And felt the excruciating pain as the copper top bullet entering his face, slammed him against the freezer before sending him to oblivion. Hearing the explosion from the gun caused the store owner to become even more frigid with the concessions of the six shots he heard. In an even greater panic, he backed away from the counter even more until he wasn't able to back up anymore because his back had met the plated glass window; he kept his hands in the air.

When a few seconds had elapsed, and he still did not see the man dressed in white, his courage was building with thoughts which told him to run from the store. He moved an inch, but then seen the man in white and quickly ran back to his position when the man in white walked back down the aisle towards him. Although the man wore a mask, the store owner dropped his head as the man approached. When the man spoke, the store owner lifted his head yet only far enough to see the man lips moving behind the mask. "You see anything?"

Violently the owner shook his head from side to side, "Me no peaky englay! . . . Me no peaky englay!"

Gizmo, wondering what was taking his brother so long to come from the store was now standing at the window looking down twenty-one stories below when he seen a bunch of people gathering and talking excitedly as they ran up the street towards the corner. "Yo, something's happening outside," he said informing the rest of the men.

"What?" Jahborn said coming, joining him at the window to see for himself. Curious as well, A.W. walked up beside them. Staring out of the window they all saw even more people now talking and pointing as they rushed toward the corner.

"Whatever it is," Jahborn said, "It's on the corner since that's where everybody's running to."

"Yeah, and that's where the store is," A.W. said with a premonition. "And that's where my brother went, I'ma go check it out," Gizmo said breaking away from them at the window.

"Hold up, wait for me!" Jahborn said as Gizmo rushed out of the apartment door.

"I'm coming too," A.W. yelled running behind both men who were already in the hallway. Too impatient to wait for the elevator, they took the stairway, taking the steps five and six at a time, and sometime whole flights. When they reached the bottom landing they were out of breath yet it did not hinder them from proceeding as they mixed in with the crowd of people who were still gathering and running towards the corner to see what had happened.

When the men reached the corner they could hear the sounds of sirens in the close distance as they pushed people aside and out of their way who was blocking the entrance to the store. Walking to the back, they saw Snoop on the floor lying next to the cooler. Since he no longer had a face they were only able to identify him through the clothes he had on. "No! No! No! Naw Man!" Gizmo hollered in anguish when he seen his brother Snoop lying on the floor. Outraged he began kicking down shelves and knocking food products to the floor. He had kicked out the freezer door window when Jahborn and A.W., feeling his pain, as well as their own, grabbing him by the shoulders and arms tried to calm him down, pulling him from the store before the police arrived.

Crying in great, big, body racking sobs, Gizmo repeated over and over, "What am I gonna tell my mom's? Huh, what the fuck am I gonna tell my mom's?"

CHAPTER ELEVEN

The surveillance of the one guy who had killed Daryle and then returned to the scene had leaded him to the trail of at least sixteen other men. Through his surveillance he had been able to distinguish the flunkies from the real shot callers, the soldiers from the major players. Due to his encounters with them, their numbers were now dwindling slowly. He had also observed a lone white man amongst them, thinking this peculiar, he pegged the white guy as their drug connect or possibly someone who had mob ties. Eager to discern the role the white guy played in the scheme of things Junior followed him one day from a meeting he had had with one of the guy's who drove a Lexus.

When the white guy's car had stopped in front of a public school in Harlem, where to Junior's surprise, the man had picked up a very light skin black woman and her daughter, Junior realized that there was more to this than met the eyes. The white guy had dropped the woman and the little girl off at their home and continued riding out of the neighborhood. Junior followed him still which lead him to the suburban, residential area that was known for being racially bias. In fact, close to fifteen years ago two black youths, experiencing car trouble, stopped for help, only instead of getting help, out of nowhere a gang of white youths appeared brandishing tire irons, bats and chains, who were being egged on by the adult whites who telling them to show the niggas they were in the wrong neighborhood, stood by and watched the fiasco. It then was reported that one black youth, out of fear tried to make a run for it, and as a result of this had been run over by another car, and died instantly, while the second black youth was being beaten beyond recognition. Several years later a mob boss, John Gotti, who also became a news media celebrity, had carved out a piece of this same area for himself, but was now doing a life sentence in Marion Federal Prison.

Using State-of-the-Art binoculars Junior observed the white guy as his car pulled into the driveway of a house where at the time a white woman and a teenage boy standing outside had met him. From the reunion it wasn't hard to discern that this was the white guy's family. Putting two and two together Junior mused as he wondered just what the white woman would do if she learned that hubby had a mistress on the side, a black one at that. A few seconds later Junior learned just how much the area was still racially motivated when the people walking by kept staring at him sitting behind the wheel of his car. Having this bit of information to store, he quickly drove off.

He also realized he no longer had the element of surprise on his side regarding the men he stalked. They were wide awoke now and armed to the teeth. Several nights ago, from a distance he had even witness them engage in what he surmised to be a drug war with some other drug dealers. He sat and watched in utter fascination as the men he stalked slaughtered their rivals, who really didn't have a chance. Miraculously, two of the people had managed to escape. It had been then, smiling, Junior had gotten an idea. He really didn't care for either group because of what they represented, but he knew that to really know his prey he had to get into their minds—to think as they thought. And in light of their drug war, like a drug dealer, he intended to exploit the weaknesses of his competitors and consolidate his assets. He had followed the two rival survivors and only after making the necessary provisions did he contact them, yet never in person, always by phone or through the use of a stranger walking the streets. Quite naturally, at first they were suspicious of him, this stranger who wanted to help them because he told them that they had something in common which was a mutual enemy. Once he had proven to them it was not a trap, their fears had been allayed and Junior moved on to faze two of his plan.

The Ghetto Soldier was sitting inside of his customized van drinking coffee. It was blistering hot outdoors and twice as suffocating inside the van with the air conditioner turned off. It was now three o'clock in the morning and he was pulling a double shift of surveillance. His black van was parked down the street from a club called the Tunnel. Had he known the mark he followed, whom at the time didn't seem to be in a festive mood, not to mention the late hour he had entered the club, was going to be inside for as long as he had, he would have paid the admission and went in behind him. He knew it was what he would do the next time his surveillance lead him to such places.

Unique, Infinite, Flavor, Hot Tee, Atomic Bomb, Brice, Raheem, A.W. and Gizmo were all seated at their reserved tables, and had been waiting on Jahborn who arrived no more than an hour ago. He now sat at the head of one end of the table while his brother Unique sat at the other. Each man had a drink of his choice sitting in front of him. Their facial expressions, grim and intense, told of the mood they were in.

People who had partied with them at other times in this same club, picking up on their vibes now, stayed clear of their tables. Women, eyeing them from the bar counter and other surrounding tables, made a point of making themselves visibly seen in the hopes that at the end of their meeting or whatever it was they was having, the men would seek them out.

Several hours ago two male notoriety rap artists from Jersey entered the club, walked up and into the DJ's booth, and said two words to him before they commenced to punch him in the face and all about his body. It was later learned that this was done because they had given the DJ their new album to check out that had not as yet been released, but mischievously; the DJ had been playing their album in the club for the public before it had even been released to the radio stations.

As if it was a reflection of his mood the DJ was now spinning the record, "Nobody does it better," by Nate Dogg and Warren Gee.

Unique tapped his glass on top of the table and then spoke up, "I called this meeting tonight because I wanted to commend all of you on the fine job we did a few weeks ago on Blackseed's ass, which only confirmed my first thoughts which was that as a team we can get shit done quicker and better."

"But the nigga got away again," Infinite said.

"Man, that nigga got nine lives—what can I say?" Unique replied, "Except the fact that in spite of the fact that he got away I believe the nigga is finished. He's through dealing. He didn't know we was gonna bring it as ugly to him like we did. Now his ass has run into hiding. I doubt if the big bad motherfucker will come out in the open again, cause if he do his ass will be out," smiling, Unique raised his glass, "I propose a toast." The men all around the tables raised their glasses.

"Now that we got Blackseed's spot I want my brother and his peeps to know that they can put their work up in the spot with ours. But we're only going to be pushing weight out of it," he intoned, looking down at the end of the table at Jahborn, "And if y'all ain't holding like that, I'll front you until you get your paper weight up. And no, I haven't forgotten about your issue with the Jamaicans, it's just that since they hadn't posed an immediate threat to you I propose we get this new spot established and then they will be next on our agenda."

"Yo, but what about this nigga running around out here like he's Charles Bronson, the vigilante and shit?" Atomic Bomb said which was also the concern of every man at the tables.

"Good point. I checked into that too and at first I thought it was Everlasting people who moved on Jahborn's peeps, but it's not, so now I'm beginning to think it's the same nigga they be talking 'bout on T.V. and the news. If it is, and since he thinks its hunting season on all ballers, I say we seek this nigga out so we can get him before he can get to anymore of us."

This topic now drew comments from the rest of the men. "Word's life, I wonna push that nigga's wig back to the white meat."

"For real though, the nigga's running around out here like he's the predator, but if I ever come across the nigga I'ma play Danny Glover on his ass—for real though."

"Yo, I say we find out who this nigga is and where he is, and come down on his ass like we did Blackseed."

"Yeah, like a ton of bricks."

"We gotta put word out on them streets and offer some kind of reward, you know?"

"Yeah, and have our police contact to start earning some of that money he be getting—greedy bastard," Infinite said.

"Yo, as y'all know, I'm still doing my thing upstate, but yo, that nigga killed my workers, and Snoop was my dog, so I gotta see this nigga and set the record straight."

"What if it's more than one nigga?"

"Man, according to the news, this nigga works alone."

"Man I don't care how many peeps he's moving with, he's gotta be had."

"Yo God, we just gotta trap that nigga off, that's all. And we gotta stay strap, and keep our eyes open and watch each other's back."

The men continued their discussion and drinking.

CHAPTER TWELVE

Junior had turned the spare bedroom Daryle once used into a study room and workplace. Shelves along side the wall were crammed with books like, William Cooper's '*Behold the Pale Horse*', '*Native Son*', by Richard Wright, '*From Superman to Man*', by J.A. Rogers, '*Color Confrontation*', by Dr. Frances Cress Welsing, and books by other black urban writers like Walter Mosely, Johnnie Sease, Donald Goines, and Charles Avery Harris.

A computer and its printer sat on an art deco desk in front of the book shelf. Because the room was also used as a gym, eighty, ninety, and hundred pound dumbbells laid in neat rows beneath a workout bench which held 315lbs of weight in its rack.

Junior worked out religiously five times a week, because of this discipline he engaged in sex on twice a week with his wife and found that this rigid regimentation kept both him and his wife in the ready for love making, as well as a greater appreciation of it when they got it. The fact that it was initiated when she least expected, was the thing that kept it exciting. The room was now being used as a workplace as Junior sat at an exceedingly long table that extended from one end of the room's wall to the next. The top of the table was laced with a black velvet cloth. Laying atop the table in neat rows was a PK19; a gun cleaning kit, and twin, seventeen shot Glock handguns, their levers were suspended back, caught on latches, exposing their empty chambers and oily barrels. A six shot riot shotgun with a black rubber hand-grip handle laid disassembled in several parts, and beside this was a re-curve Bear Bow with an infrared scope attached, the scope operated off of heat sensors. In the next row beneath this laid Twin Desert Eagles and twin black Calicos, beside them were two Kevlar bulletproof vests which lay on top of one another. Beside them laid a Halfner-schnit Compound Cross Bow; because its arrows held the velocity of releasing over 350lbs of pressure when shot, it required the use of an electronic wench to crank its powerful bow string.

The wench was affixed to the bow's base. A night-star scope was attached to its bridge, the screen on the scope was green, and its power of vision was generated by the light from the stars at night. Bowie knives of various sizes lay next to the sheaves that they went inside. In the third and final row lay an assortment of electronic surveillance equipment: a 120 channel police scanner, a micro-size voice disguiser that required no modular hookups. It lay in cushions atop the box. Beside this laid a bumper beeper tracking device. It was only three inches big, and was used to track a car, allowing the person to follow that car without being observed. It also gave directional information of up to five miles in any direction. This unit device used magnets or two sided adhesive material that could be placed on the underside of a car, or better yet, inside a car's bumper for better concealment. Next to this was an Infinity Harmonic Bug, often referred to as a hook-switch, or a bypass, or a third wire tap. This small transmitter; a clever device, turned any telephone receiver into a listening device, even while the phone was on its hook. To eavesdrop all one simply had to do was call the mark's phone number and then remotely activate the Infinity transmitter just before the phone rang. Junior was like a big kid when it came to these toys of his, and could be engrossed for hours experimenting with them. A pair of fake Tiffany lamps stood next to a clock radio and a thirteen inch color T.V. They all would be used in a gift ruse which would allow him to monitor those he sought.

Ever since the last attack he made against his prey it appeared that they all had went into hiding. And whenever they were out in the open they deliberately, or unwittingly, flocked around the innocent, making it difficult for Junior to strike against them. When they moved, it was like hyenas, they traveled in packs. It was then he realized the pursuit of his quarries would be adventurous, and he looked forward to the hunt. Like eels, they appeared to be very slippery. He surmised that the toll of their lifestyle and all the dirt they had done to others dictated it, and had made them all naturally paranoid. He noted how their behavior, when out in public, as something as simple as getting out of a car was done with extra precaution. Their flittering eyes would swiftly dot up and down both ends of the streets as if they knew they were being watched. Junior liked the idea that they were all uncomfortable now, his actions had disturbed their groove and they couldn't enjoy the lifestyle they had worked so hard to have and had become accustom to.

A pair of Pursuit 2000 glasses pinched the tip of Junior's nose as he sat in a worn, yet comfortable leather chair, tinkering with a concealed wall plug transmitter. The pinhole in its center concealed a miniature microphone. He was transferring it into the LCD light on a smoke alarm detector, while listening to a jazz radio station. This electronic unit he worked on could pick up and transmit sounds, words and even whispers from any room. The loud jazz music playing now helped him relax and allowed him to concentrate better. Just then he heard the faint ringing of a telephone, pausing in his work, he looked around the room, the ringing was definitely not coming from the phone a few feet away from him. Several seconds later he heard a loud knock at the door, and responded as equally loud, "Yeah?"

"Daddy, mommy said you got a call on your private line," Kim said from the other side of the door.

"Tell her I'm coming," he said.

It had been during surveillance on the white guy that Junior began to pick up bad vibes about him. Upon closer scrutiny he got the feeling that the white guy was a cop or once had been, it was all in his mannerism, so he took down the guy's license plate numbers and made a few calls to have it checked out. "Tell her I'll be right there," he said placing his tools careful on the table. Maybe it was the call he had been waiting for he thought leaving the room.

Kim was standing next to her mother, who was lying across the bed when Junior, in bear feet and wearing draw—string sweatpants, and a white tank top rushed into the room and snatched up the phone that was still ringing. "Hello."

"Hold on," Junior said snapping his finger for Karla to pass him pen and paper. She did, but not before giving him the evil eye.

"Okay, shoot."

"ThenameisDonaldPataki;he'sinthedrugdepartment—fourteen years on the force. Married, wife name is Gloria and they have a fourteen year old son together name Donald Jr."

"Un," Junior grunted.

"He's got a partner; Theodore Giuliani. He's been brought up on three charges of extortion—shaking down drug dealers. For the last six months he's been under investigation—unbeknown to him, of course."

"Well from these last few weeks according to the unsavory elements I've seen his partner Pataki hanging round with I'd say he's up to his neck in dirt too."

"Another lost soul gone astray."

"Chose the crooked path."

"Yeah, and get this, Pataki himself has had seven charges lodged against him. Four by noted drug dealers for extortion and robbery, and three separate charges of sexual assault, all by working girls."

"Prostitutes?"

"Yep. And personally I think he's the luckiest guy in the world, that, or he's very clever."

"Why you say that?"

"Because before any of the drug dealers could testify against him before an Internal Affair committee, each one of them was gunned down in a cold blood by rival drug gangs."

"And the girls?"

"Mysteriously disappeared without a trace."

Junior's countenance suddenly changed, deep furrows appeared on his dark forehead as he quietly took in this information.

"You still there?"

"Yeah—I think I got the picture now, and I can take it from here."

"See you around."

"Yeah. Oh and hey . . . ."

"Yeah?"

"Thanks!"

Hanging up the phone, Junior ripped the page from the pad, and asked Karla, "What's for dinner?"

"It was Kim's turn to cook today so you'll have to ask her." Hearing this made him reflect on how, as of late he had noticed that she had been acting funny lately. And speculated that it must have been that time of the month. Looking around him for Kim who at this time had already left the room, he walked through the house and passed by his office room and noticed he had mistakenly left the door open. Only now it seemed to be closed a lot further than he recalled having left it. Walking into the living room he found Kim sitting on the couch with her back to him looking at the television. He noted how she hadn't turned around to face him though there was really nothing of interest on the screen. "What's for dinner my clever Boo Bear?" He asked, seeing her smile before it disappeared when she turned around to face him. "Steak, string beans, macaroni and cheese, and I went out earlier and bought your sprite soda."

"Good, cause I'm starving," he turned to leave just as Kim jumped up from the couch, "I'll fix your food for you now Daddy. Mommy's hungry too. We've been waiting for you to come out your study room so we could eat. After all, this is the weekend where we're supposed to eat together as a family, right?" Kim said slipping into the kitchen ahead of him.

"Right you are Lady," Junior said, realizing he had forgotten. He had made a rule that every other Sunday that they sat down and ate dinner together. Closing his office room door completely now, he went to the bathroom to wash up. When he returned to the dining room his family was already seated at the table with food in front of them. Everyone bowed their heads as he said grace. Several minutes into their meals, Karla said, "So how did you like the sermon the preacher gave in church today?"

"Well, I liked what he was saying about revelations twelve, verse eighteen—how he related it to all the big shots up on Capitol Hill."

"Me too daddy," Kim smiled, 'I like what he was saying about, how since Satan can't get to god himself he use people up on Capitol Hill to do his dirty work for him, and how he wait for people to get weaken when they come out of church and turn them into double dealing deacons, primsy pimping preachers and all that other stuff."

"Yeah well, I liked the way he was talking about heathens, and speaking of heathens," Karla said to Junior, "These last few Sundays I've been noticing how that heathen Patricia Gloglen keep looking and smiling at you. And don't be playing like you haven't noticed either," she said a bit beefy. Smiling, Kim dropped her head embarrassed for her father. Junior knew what Karla was getting at about the woman Patricia, he had noticed it himself.

"Maybe that heathen thinks you're a good candidate to take care of them eleven kids of hers," Karla's mentioning of kids made Kim remember something. "Guess what daddy?"

"What Lady?"

"I'm going to have a brother or sister soon." Looking at her he then looked at Karla who was now looking at Kim as if to say she had a big mouth. Realizing her husband was still staring at her she averted her eyes and smiled.

"Well?" Junior said.

Karla shook her head up and down.

"Well, when were you going to tell me?" But before she could speak he said, "It better be a boy. Cause since Daryle passed away I've been out numbered here. I remember when I use to be the first to know things around here, now I'm the last to know."

"I, not too long ago found out myself so Junior please."

"Still I—"

"Daddy, if it's a boy lets name him Daryle."

Karla liking this idea but also felt that their first son should always be named after his father. After dinner they played cards for quarters, since Junior won all their money, to which they suspected he was cheating, they bought the game to a close. From there they all piled into the car and went to Carvel's next to the Restoration Center in Bedfordstuyvesant and had ice cream.

To most of the people who earned their bread and butter on the streets by any means necessary, it was believed that Manhattan was the Mecca of the drug trade, what with all its drug trafficking which dated back to the late 50's for most of the blacks. But little did many know or take notice that on the flip side of that coin lay the borough of Brooklyn. A place considered the most poverty stricken of all the five boroughs in the city of New York. No one ever considered the possibility that it was deliberately made to look that way, nor did anyone seem to remember that it was traditionally the first home of most gangsters who migrated here dating back to the roaring 20's. Nor did anyone seem to make a connection of the major drug transportation with the fact that this borough had a shipping dock.

It was Tuesday, 4:30 in the evening. A teenage boy stood on top of a three story family house roof, shielding his eyes from the bright blazing sun as he looked up into the sky. He whistled loudly to the New York City pigeons flying high in a circular formation above his head. Down below on the streets people could be seen mingling, going to and fro. Teenage girls and guys dressed in baggy jeans and oversize Tee-shirts, standing near the corner phone booths kidded each other as they laughed and talked; it was the prelude, their modus operandi of getting pass first base so they could move on to the next level of courtship.

Women pushing baby carriages strolled up and down both ends of the street. Unemployed men leaned against parked cars with beers in their hands, conspired together on ways to catch their next criminal case. Women wearing two piece skirt suits with white low top sneakers, which hinted that they were on their way home from a hard day's work, ignored the comments made by the men standing on the corners. Other domestic women, wearing tight shorts and tank tops could be seen buying Italian ices from a man pushing an icy cart. Teens with blood shot eyes from smoking weed could be seen standing in front of the corner stores.

A man, young in age, walked down the street of Tabscott in Brownsville, carrying a brown shopping bag. While another man, much older, at the same time, walked out the doors of his three family brownstone house, carrying a brown shopping bag too. Descending the steps of his building the old man very casually proceeded to walk down the street. After a short time he was coincidentally only a few yards behind the young man. Several seconds later they both entered the bodega on the corner, one seconds behind the other. The store was semi crowded and each man took a separate aisle to walk to the coolers at the back of the store. The owner in the front of the store behind the counter recognized the old man as a regular customer, he knew his wife, kids and grand kids who often frequent his store. He also knew that the old man lived only a few buildings down. But the other man he had never seen before, but from the attire the man had on he doubted if he would have to watch him to make sure he didn't steal anything, and therefore paid neither man any attention.

In the back of the store the younger man sat his shopping bag down by his feet as he slid open the freezer door and reached inside. It was at this time that older man, approaching from behind placed his shopping bag next to the identical one that was already on the floor. As the young man closed the freezer door with a container of orange juice in his hand, he mistakenly picked up the second shopping bag instead of his own and then made his way to the front of the store. After purchasing a pack of chewing gum he made his way out of the store.

The old man paid for his can of tomato juice while making small talk with his friend behind the counter and then walked out of the store. Out on the streets he did not walk like he was in a rush but casually, with an old man walk he paced back down the street with a shopping bag and made his way back into his brownstone.

Neither the young or old man bothered to look into each other's bags to make sure everything was straight, intuitively they knew both counts of the money and drugs would be correct. Their relationship was based on a mutual trust and the both knew as long as it stayed that way they would continue to do business together. Another interesting thing which tied to two men together was that the old man whose name was Cut, was also the godfather of the younger man whose name was Unique. They had been doing business for years together in the transactions of both dope and coke. It was only because Unique was the old man's god son that the old man dealt with him personally instead of letting him deal with his underlings to which he had for such occasions. Unique had long agreed to never reveal who his connect was or he would be cut off. And although Cut was Unique's godfather, deep down inside he believed he was also his biological father as well. And though he had never uttered a word about this he believed that his god son suspected the same as he grew curious over the years as to why the old man treated him extra special.

Walking around the corner on Legion, Unique entered his car.

CHAPTER THIRTEEN

Brice and Justice were both seated at a table in Shabazz's restaurant located on 116th and 8th avenue. It was nine o'clock at night and they both had just finished working their shift at the spot they had taken away from Blackseed.

When Blackseed's coup against Unique had failed he had done the next best thing—he moved his workers off the streets and into a second floor apartment in one of the buildings on the block. Tonight was Justice first time working in the spot since he had been promised a job in East New York that never came through. But he was in good spirits tonight due to the money he was now making. He had seen coke before but nothing in the amount he had seen in the spot, he had been surrounded by so much coke that it made him feel like Tony Montana. Because they worked the shift together, Brice had showed him the ropes; he learned that there were 31/2 grams in an eight ball, 28 grams in an ounce, 2 ounces plus six grams in a sixty-two, and thirty-five ounces plus twenty free grams in a kilo. This knowledge made Justice somehow feel different now, like he knew something now that the guys he normally hung out with didn't know. They were still on the street corners selling three dollar bottles, but since he teamed up with Unique, Brice and the rest of the crew, he was now working in a spot breaking down kilos.

A waiter placed two glasses of water and two menus in front of them at their table. They were seated about seven tables away from the establishment's plated glass window. From their location they could see cars passing in either direction in the streets, as well as people walking up and down the block.

Shabazz restaurant was unusually crowded for a Thursday night, and people were still standing, waiting to be seated as a steady drone of conversation from the many different tables permeated the air of the large room. Waiters carrying trays of food, cash, credit cards receipts, and drinks bustled to and fro across the room as if they were in a hurry.

Although Justice lived in Brooklyn, which was only one borough away, he had never been to Harlem before, and knew that had it not been for his job in the spot in Manhattan, he would have never known about Shabazz's since he never left Brooklyn. In fact it had been Brice who had brought him here, when, while working, he had told Brice he wanted to celebrate the fact that he had a job and was making money now and that he was down with a set tight clique. Until the recent takeover Justice had not been brought in on any of the happenings since everything was on a need to know basis. He was also aware of the fact that the guys from Manhattan didn't like nor trust guys from Brooklyn—but now he was in. He hadn't thought it would happen but it did, and he intended to show them his appreciation through his loyalty.

The .380 Taurus handgun on his hip beneath his shirt felt clammy against his sweaty skin, but he was on top of things and sure that Brice who was holding a gat identical to his, was feeling the same way. A waiter wearing his brown and white uniform, and a promotional smile approached their table, "May I take your orders now?"

"Yeah, I'll have the veal parmesan and spaghetti," said Brice.

"Yeah, and bring me," Justice paused looking down at the menu, " . . . I want a steak well-done, scramble eggs and toast." He concluded. What had appealed to him when Brice told him about Shabazz's was that you could order whatever you wanted, breakfast at dinner time, lunch for breakfast or a combination of them all at the same time.

"And what would you gentlemen like to drink?"

"A big glass of lemonade."

"Yeah, and I'll have a Pepsi," Brice added. And then said to Justice, "I thought we were celebrating man?"

"Oh yeah, word. Yo, y'all got champagne here, right?"

"Yes," the waiter nodded and then pointed to the beverage section in Justice's menu.

"Bring us a bottle of Moet, chilled. And we want it now."

"Will that be all?"

"Yeah."

Taking their menus the waiter left to fill their orders. As they watched the waiter's back departing, the men turned in their seats as their eyes searched the room in hopes of finding some single available females they could bag before Unique and the rest of the crew got there. Because of this neither man took notice of the 1999 pink champagne color Toyota Camry that had pulled up, double parking in front of the restaurant.

Turning the volume down on the radio in the car Junior flipped open his phone and dialed seven numbers, when the other end picked up several rings later, he spoke briefly, "There's two of them—alone, that I'm sure you'll recognize—Shabazz's restaurant—116th and 8th." Dropping the phone on the seat next to him Junior turned the car's radio volume back up and drove off.

Residue now lay in the bottle of Moet that had been polished off by the men by the time the waiter now brought them their food, "Can I get you gentlemen anything else?"

"Naw, that'll be all for now," the men laughed feeling a buzz from the champagne.

"Well my name is Bobby," the waiter said tapping his name tag. He liked when these kind of guys came to eat, he knew they were ballers (hustlers) and that they usually left a big tip, trying to empress one another, "And if there's anything else the either of you might want or need just give me a call," the waiter said and walked away.

"Are you in the yellow pages?" Justice wise-cracked as the effect of the champagne he'd drunken so fast made his head feel light. The waiter half turn back around to face them, "Excuse me?"

"Nothing . . . nothing," Brice said, waving him off with his hand.

"Dad-da boy Bobby!" Justice boomed and them both men cracked up with laughter.

Almost ten minutes later a short brown skin muscular man entered Shabazz's. The guy's name was Skip, and he had a street reputation for putting in work of the violent nature. Standing just beyond the threshold of the diner he began looking around the large room as if in search of someone he'd suppose to have met there. His eyes stopped on a table several yards away and his whole expression turned evil. He saw two men sitting at their table eating. He recognized one of the men as Brice.

They had met only once before and the encounter hadn't been pleasant. He didn't recognize the second man but it didn't matter, but he had to be sure that the guy he was looking at was Brice. Skip then convinced one of the waiters' to let him use the bathroom although it was against the establishment policy. On his way to the bathroom Skip passed by Brice's table several feet away. He stared at him with an ice grill but Brice hadn't looked up to acknowledge him. Skip was sure it was Brice as he passed his table now on his way out of the restaurant. Just then Brice tuned out what Justice was saying and looked up, as Justice chattered on, "Word man, the bitch name is Monica, and I be digging her back out now on the regular, and I j—" Justice paused when he realize he no longer had Brice's attention. Looking up he followed Brice's eyes that was now on the back of a guy exiting the doors of the restaurant. "What's up?—what's wrong yo?"

"Naw, it ain't nothing, it's just that that cat leaving outta here right now look a lot like a nigga named Skip whose down with that nigga Blackseed we tried to stretch."

Quickly, and without warning Justice stood up from their table, "Shit, we're both strapped, let's go see if it's the nigga." But before he could move away Brice caught him by the wrist and pulled him back down to his chair, "Naw, that ain't him, chill. Both of them niggas is in hiding somewhere."

"Damn man, I don't know why y'all didn't call me so I could have got in on that action too."

Smiling, Brice told himself, if there was one thing he had to confess, it was that Brooklyn niggas were gung-ho which was a good asset to have around you when there was beef. Aloud he said, "Don't sweat it yo, cause in this game they'll be plenty of opportunities, so you'll get your chance." The men resumed their conversation where Justice was telling him about a chick name Monica and how she was a freak with a capital 'F'.

When Skip sensed Brice had been looking in his direction, he kept his head straight as he walked out of the doors.

Ten minutes had passed before the unarguable blending of lemonade and champagne, taking its toll, began attacking Justice bladder. Standing from the table he said, "Hold it down lord, I'm going to the bathroom—be right back." As soon as Justice left Brice reached for his cell phone to call Unique to find out what was taking him and Infinite so long to get there. They had told him that they would meet him and Justice there because they wanted to talk to him about something. They had also given him some money to hold but hadn't told him what is was for.

Pulling the phone from his pants, its battery section got snagged on his pocket and fell to the floor. "Shit!" He cursed as he bend down beneath the table to pick them up. It was at this moment that Blackseed, tall and dark skin entered the diner holding a seventeen shot Glock in his hand down by the side of his leg. He frowned when he no longer seen Brice, he knew he had seen him sitting at a table no more than a few seconds ago. He had spied on him through the plated window glass before coming in. He thumped the safety latch off the gun and then began walking towards the table he had last seen Brice sitting at. Just then a waiter was about to approach Blackseed to inform him that there were no more available seats, that is, until he noticed the gun in Blackseed's hand, and the words then froze on his lips as he scrambled away, too afraid to even shout for help out of fear of getting shot. It was at this moment that Brice sat back up straight in his seat, the batteries in one hand and his phone in the other. Blackseed seen him then.

Snapping the batteries back into place Brice looked up and seen Blackseed, the expression on Brice's face now was as if he was now looking at his father but knew that it couldn't be since his father had died over twenty years ago. Quickly, he threw the phone to the side and reached for his gun. Blackseed raised his gun, pointed at Brice and began squeezing the trigger while walking closer to the table. In less than a minute eleven shots had rung off, digging and mutilating Brice's face before Blackseed had sense enough to release his finger from the trigger. Somewhere in his mind he knew he had to save some bullets because the guy who had been with Brice was still somewhere in the restaurant. The patrons in Shabazz's at this time had knocked over their tables and dove behind them for cover. Women were hollowing, screaming and crying. The waiters, lying on the floor, covered their ears in an effort to block out the deafening sounds. Brice, who had died instantly when the first bullet tore into his face, ripping cartilage, had landed itself in a part of his brain responsible for the motor impulse, was now leaned back, as if even in death, with the will to defy Blackseed, Brice, even in death did not fall from his seat. As Blackseed took quick steps towards the diner's people on the floor covered their eyes hoping it would assure the gunman he had no reason to kill them because they had not seen him.

Justice was zipping up his zipper in the bathroom when he heard the report of gunshots fired. Snatching his gun from his waist he rushed out of the bathroom brandishing his gat which caused the people getting up from the floor to lie back down.

Skip, sitting behind the wheel of a black BMW with its motor running idle seen his boss exiting the restaurant urged him on. Rushing now Blackseed closed the distance between him and the car awaiting him across the street and thought he was hallucinating when he seen dozens of police cars coming in every direction. As this was taking place, somewhere in the recessive part of his brain he wondered how they had gotten there so quickly. Skip had pulled off before Blackseed had got in the car completely, when they seen that the cops had the streets blocked they jumped on the sidewalk, knocking down garbage cans and anything else in their way as they drove. People on the sidewalk ran out into the streets for safety. Reaching the corner Skip rammed into a squadron of police cars in an effort to break through their barricade. When it didn't work he threw the gear in reverse and backed up on the sidewalk again to try something else. It was then that the police standing outside of their cars with guns in hand interpreted the collision as a threat to their lives and began to open fire on the two men in the car.

Pataki arrived on the scene twenty minutes later; he had heard the call come over the squad car radio. He had been headed for the same restaurant to pick up his pay-off money from Unique and Infinite, only what he didn't know was that they had given the money to Brice to give to him who they intended to make his contact from now on. When Pataki heard about what had happened and the description given of the culprit, he thought it fitted the same description of the guy the news media had labeled as the Ghetto Soldier. And when he heard that the man and his accomplice were both dead, he told himself, "There goes my promotion." Only when he viewed the bodies in the car and seen that it was Blackseed he didn't know whether he should be happy or sad.

In the aftermath it was learned that the police had received an unanimous tip about what was going to go down only they arrived on the scene too late. Only one person knew that the time of their arrival had been just right.

CHAPTER FOURTEEN

When Junior had followed Unique to his home out in Queens he had been duly impressed when Unique's car drove up into the driveway of a Victorian style home which clearly looked the most lavish from the outside and appeared to be the most expensive on the block. It had reminded him of the house he and his family had intended to purchase, but then Daryle had gotten killed and that had changed everything, not changed it but prolonged it, he still intended to buy a home for his family because he felt they deserved it.

Trisha, wearing matching silk pants and blouse, was standing at the plated glass window in her living room watering her plants. She had seen people talking to their plants before and at the moment was doing the same thing when she seen a brown van with the words on the side that read: 'Fire and Safety Department', written in big bold white letters, stop in front of her house. She paused in her conversation as she seen a man getting out of the van, he held an uncanny resemblance to Blackseed who worked for her man Unique, but who later became an avowed enemy. Because she was attracted to men of dark complexion she thought he was attracted. She had told herself that it was natural for any red blooded woman who was committed to one man to be attracted to another man, just as long as she did not act on that attraction—everything was fine. However, she knew that the man she was looking at now could not be Blackseed since the news said he had been gunned down and killed in his car by the police. So when she seen this man in his beige cap and beige uniform, which she felt shone brightly in the afternoon sun and contrasted nicely with his dark complexion, walking up the passageway leading to her front door, in her mind she began to formulate the dialogue she would use this time to tell him, as she had done so many others, who had made the mistake of going to the wrong house.

The UPS man and other delivery men had done the same thing on many other occasions to the point that she had thought of putting a sign out in front of her house that said; Try the house next door. When she had become friend's with a female, of a couple who lived down the street who were almost as young as they were, the two women often got together on the phone or in person where they would swap stories about their encounters and how neither of them had come across a delivery man attractive enough for them to invite in for tea, coffee or some other type of refreshment.

As the chimes of Trisha's doorbell rung loudly through the house she advanced to the door and opened it casually, "Yes, may I help you?" She said looking up into the tall man's face. Junior stood before her in his starched uniform and cap with a clip board in his hand. "Good afternoon," he said tapping the bogus name tag which shown his picture clipped to his shirt, "I'm the chief inspector from the Fire and Safety Department."

Trisha's eyes held onto the name tag for a second and then veered to the clip board where she recognized the addresses to the houses beside hers, going in either direction. Her eyes then raised and held back with Junior's. Damn, this nigga's handsome—thick and chocolate like milkshake, she thought.

"We're checking to see how many residents are following the guidelines of our fire and safety policy to which had been agreed to upon signing the mortgage papers to their homes. May I come in?"

Liking what she seen, Trisha smiled, and was surprised at herself for boldly holding eye contact with him for so long without being the first to break it. At the moment Unique was out in the streets conducting his business, and she couldn't wait to get on the phone to call her friend down the street to tell her about the hunk she had in her house. "Yes, come in."

Junior recognized the look in this woman's eyes; he'd seen it many times before in the eyes of others, and for the first time hoped he could make it work for him. As he entered the house he reached down and picked up a small red fire extinguisher.

Trisha admitted to herself that she hadn't even seen it there until he had reached down to pick it up.

"Fine house you have here," Junior said standing in the living room looking around him. This room, as he imagined all the others were, laced with the best quality furniture.

"Thank you, Trisha said and then blushed like a little girl, not knowing what had come over her. She attributed it to the fact that outside of Unique, this guy was the first man who had ever stepped foot into this house.

"It would be a shame to one day see it all go up in smoke," he said waving his hand. His strong velvety voice then asked, "Do you have smoke alarms?"

Though Trisha had heard him speaking the trance she was in had eluded her from responding immediately which prompted Junior to repeat himself, "Excuse me Mrs. But do you have smoke alarms?

She heard him clearly this time, "Ah, no, yes, I mean, I'm not married. And yes, of course we have smoke alarms—two of them. One right above your head and the other is in the bedroom." Her conscious then caused her to question the way her last statement might have sounded.

Junior reached into a small pouch strapped to his waist and removed a small screwdriver; turning his back now he reached up and popped the face off the smoke detector. Trisha's pulse began to race fast as if she'd just ran five miles, when her eyes veered down to Junior's rump and liking the way his pants was hugging his ass. As she continued to stare she felt her clitoris jumping, as her thoughts flashed on the night before last where she had fingered herself, it had been the first time ever for her. She had been horny and those strong urges were coming back to her now as she realized she was lusting for this man mixed with a ping of guilt. She told herself it was all Unique's fault.

He was so caught up in his business out in the streets that he had been neglecting her sexually, it was going on two months. She had told herself that the two of them would have to talk. She watched Junior as he removed a cigarette lighter from his pocket and flicked the fire underneath the alarm. Seconds later they both heard a piercing, thrilling sound coming from the smoke alarm. He quickly disconnected the battery and then reconnected it. Placing the face back on the alarm he said, "Well, this one seems to be in working order, let's see the next one."

Trisha led him to her bedroom, where once there, she found the urge for sex even stronger. She told herself it was all in her mind but her clitoris was still jumping and thumping double time. Junior repeated the act he had performed in the living room, only this time neither of them heard the alarm ring off. He knew it probably was just due to a dead battery and had it not been he would have found something wrong with it anyway. "Oh-oh," he said in a professional voice while forcing the detector off the wall, "looks like we got a defective smoke alarm here." Pulling another one from his pouch, pulling the paper off the sticky part, he then placed the alarm where the other one had been. "I'd hate to be asleep in this room had there been a fire."

Trisha, understanding his point and thankful for him having detected a faulty alarm, asked, "Would you care for something to drink Ted? I hope it's alright to call you by your first name?" She leered with a lascivious glare.

"Sure, I'm not that formal," Junior said looking down at her. He could tell she wasn't wearing a bra because he could see faint shadows of her dark brown nipples through her white silk blouse, and they seemed to grow more and more visibly erect each time they brushed lightly against the fabric. "And ah, as to that drink—it's against rules and regulations but I must admit that my throat it's parched," as if embarrassed, he dropped his eyes, "There's no A.C. in the company's van that I drive. And surprisingly not many in the homes I go to around here but," he looked back up into her eyes again which never left his face, "I can feel that yours is running strong and hard."

For a second Trisha had a feeling that he knew what she was feeling and because of this didn't quite know how to reply, and at the last moment decided to say something wicked. "Well I won't tell if you won't tell." This statement with its dual meaning had not gotten pass Junior either who said, "In that case my lips are sealed cause I've never been one to reveal when someone has done something nice for me."

Trisha, hesitated for a second, waiting for him to say more but when he hadn't she went into the kitchen to get him something to drink. Using this opportunity Junior quickly picked up the receiver to the bedroom phone and placed a monitor bug inside for added measures, and screwed the mouth piece back on in record timing.

As Trisha re-entered the room with the drink Junior was putting the smoke alarm with the dead battery into his pouch. Taking the drink from her hand their fingers touched yet she didn't bother to pull away to break the contact because she was too busy fighting off the urges to seduce him while at the same time she envision herself standing at the bathroom mirror at her sink wringing out her panties to which she knew by this time would have been soak and wet—only she didn't wear any.

"Thank you," Junior said after taking a healthy swallow from his drink to which he detected had been laced with liquor.

When he made no comment she said smiling, "I hope you don't mind but I took the liberty of adding a tid bit of Remy Martin to your seven up. I thought it would make your route which seem so tedious, it bit more bearable in this sweltering weather. But if you're like, because you're driving, I could fix you something a bit more platonic?" She said reaching for his glass as their fingers touched again.

"No-no, this will do just fine," Junior said and to proving his point he turned the glass up and drained it. Trisha laughed, "You see, I knew that your thirst was quint-essential."

"Yes, and in ways you could never imagine," he said handing her back the glass.

"You'd be surprised at what I can imagine," she said and then walked out of the room. Turning around she seem him following her and subconsciously felt upset that he was leaving out of the bedroom. Stopping she asked in a voice that sounded disappointing, "Is that all you're going to do?" Realizing that this to didn't sound right, she capped, "I mean, are you finished?"

"Uh, yes. With that alarm, that is. What I need to know now is, if you have a fire extinguisher on the premises?"

Trisha stared into his irresistible, Smokey bedroom eyes again, she couldn't help it, they were pulling her like a magnet. She said, "fire extinguisher?—no, we've never had one."

"Well, following a hunch I brought one along just in case, and now I'm glad I did. Normally you would have to pay for it, but because you were so nice and gorgeous I'm going to let you have it for free," he said handing it to her where they made hand contact again, "And it'll be just our little secret."

"Oh wild—thanks! And you won't have to worry—I'm good at keeping secrets too," she said now clinging the extinguisher to her bosom. Junior's intuition told him that if he didn't get out her house now he would wound up on with carpet burns from being on the floor with her. Having now seen the women of both shot-callers he had to admit that they both had good taste in women. "Once again, thanks for the drink," he said.

"It was nothing," Trisha said holding the door open for him, "But this," she said, hefting up the extinguisher, "Is everything, it can save lives—so thank you."

"My pleasure," Junior said walking out the door. In his mind he told himself he would hate if a time came where he would have to do something to her personally, she was just so pretty.

Hours later he was in the garage where his cars were kept. And with a hole's attached to a powerful water gun he water blasted the water painted letters from the sides of his van.

*   *   *

It was now two weeks later. Junior had Pataki in his visual sight. It was Wednesday, early afternoon. The sun showing no mercy beat down upon pedestrians walking along the crowded 34th street in Manhattan. Just on a hunch he had followed Pataki today, and aside from all the other places he went, it had lead him here. The way the cop's hand kept drumming on the steering wheel inside his car told Junior he was waiting for someone and was becoming impatient.

Pataki then jumped out of his car, walked to the news stand a few feet away and bought himself a snicker's candy bar. Leaning against the fender of his car he devoured the candy bar in less than a minute, only instead of throwing the candy wrapper in the trash basket a few feet away, Junior observed him rip open the paper and read something inside. Every now and then Pataki looked up. Seconds later he pulled himself up off his car and stuck the candy wrapper paper in his pocket, he then walked into the stationary store right next to the news stand. Junior, only a few yards away, watched him closely.

Less than two minutes later Pataki re-emerged from the store carrying a stamp and a small white envelope. Squinting his eyes, he looked up and down both ends of the street before climbing back into his car. And immediately began jotting down information onto his memo pad. This done, he addressed the envelope, stuck the candy wrapper inside, along with the sheet from the memo pad and sealed the envelope. Looking out of his window on the driver's side, he looked behind him and then climbed back out of his car while the cars in this busy street were stopped at a red light. Running across the street he dropped the envelope in the mailbox on the corner and made it back inside of his car before the light had turned green again.

Junior cursed under his breath when through his rear view mirror he seen a brownie traffic cop coming his way, because he was double parked he knew he had to move. The traffic light was still green and he pulled off into traffic, making a left turn at the corner. He was only going to circle the block and prayed that Pataki would still be there when he returned because within that time he also knew he could be long gone. If that happened he knew it would take some time for him to find him again since he didn't, as of yet, have a tracking device concealed somewhere on his car.

When he returned to the station he had previously been parked, he breathed a sigh of relief when he seen that Pataki was still there. Several seconds later he peeked Pataki's mistress walking down the block towards him, she had been coming from the direction where the Department of Human Services was located. He also noted that she didn't bother to wait for Pataki to open her side of the door for her, and that Pataki didn't attempt to.

When their car pulled out into traffic Junior didn't follow them in as much that he had a good idea where they were headed. Instead he climbed out of his car, ran to the news stand and bought a snickers bar. Throwing the candy in a waste basket, he carefully tore open the wrapper and read the contents within. It was a contest which told how a person could win the first prize of two million dollars, or a consolation prize of second and third place. He climbed back into his car while reading the instructions and his car veered out into traffic.

On another stake out he had observed Pataki removing the sweepstakes section from the news paper. And at that time he mused over the fact that a man like Pataki still believed in luck.

Smiling now as he drove he suddenly realized who would be receiving his rigged lamps that really weren't from Tiffany's. He also decided he would throw the alarm clock radio into the package deal too for good measures, well actually, monitoring measures.

Two weeks later Pataki was ecstatic when he received a notice from the post office informing him that he had one week to pick up the parcel package there waiting for him. Eager to learn what it was, Pataki had called the post office and had sweet talked the female clerk into describing the size and weight of the box that was there for him, and became even more excited when he was told that there were two packages there for him. Without wasting any time the very next day on his lunch break Pataki picked up his packages. Though it wasn't the two million dollars he was still shit grinning happy about the alarm clock radio and his lamps from Tiffany's. He immediately took them home placing them both in his bedroom.

CHAPTER FIFTEEN

It was nine o'clock on a Friday night, men and women both had rushed from their jobs looking for relaxation and fun, only instead of going home first their presence became a fixture inside a club called Mrs. Arizona on Atlantic Avenue in Brooklyn. Its small confines, the size of a corner grocery store, was more of a crap house than a club.

Through the fate of dice games many people became thousands of dollars richer in one night, but just as many had found themselves out of their recently obtained paychecks as well. Those unfortunate ones afraid to go home due to the fight that would ensue once their loved ones learned what had happened, could be found scrounging a drink at the bar while at the same time feasting their eyes upon the female strippers up on a small stage which offered, though pleasant, but only temporary distraction.

Just as many women frequent Arizona's as there were men, who once trying their luck at the dice, knowing, if they paid off, a strange woman would quickly become attached to their elbow as a consolation prize which came with their great fortune at the dice.

The women who frequent this club was well versed in the art of gambling, only instead of tossing the dice they allowed their looks and guile to determine their fate for the evening.

The club's atmosphere was filled with sex and deception. And anyone not wise to the game would easily be devoured. Fist fights were current but gun fights were the norm. And on many of nights the sidewalk in front of the club feasted upon the blood of some poor soul who had lost more than just his money. Most police stayed clear of this area knowing that each time they approached this place it would have to be with their guns drawn. But many off duty police officers catered to this place too.

It was the only place in Brooklyn where one could see the police officers and true thugs coming together like one nation under a groove for more than five minutes and not be ready to tear each other's hearts out. Though drugs were not sold on the premises, money, sex and drugs and violence were all rolled up into one and made available for all the daring souls who were looking for a night of fun on the edge.

Tonight the dice had frown on Gizmo, and though he had told his woman hours ago that he was on his way, the fact that he hadn't gotten there yet had nothing to do with fear or worry. He had lost over five hundred dollars on the dice game and was hoping that Raheem, his partner for the night, would be able to help him get his money back. So far Raheem was on a winning streak and had managed to put four or five hundred back into Gizmo's pocket. Raheem himself was thirty five hundred dollars ahead of the game and loved every minute of it. A crowd of men stood in a circle around the crap table, shouts of profanity blending like harmony with the loud music playing could be heard throughout the club.

Raheem, with Gizmo standing beside him, stood at the head of the crap table shaking three dice in his hand, talking loud, drawing attention to himself. The looks on the men faces told that they weren't good at losing and that Raheem was talking too much shit. The sounds of DMX, 'Stop being greedy',' blasted through the club's speakers as Raheem continued to signify, "Ah, you niggas ain't about no money—none of you niggas want no money—cause all you niggas is scared to bet, and scared money can't win no money," he said dropping the dice on the table which landed on the numbers Six, six, six.

"Shit!" someone exclaimed as Gizmo raked all the money on the table towards him and his partner. Raheem was hot tonight; there was no doubt about it. The men had changed the dice on him three times yet he continued to win.

"Place your bets, the bank's money," Raheem said picking up the dice again and shaking them in his hand. He laughed in the men faces, taunting them before his attention was distracted when he looked up on the stage and seen a stripper named Cookie. With her back to him, she bend forward and spread her ass cheeks.

"Ooooo-Weeeee!" Raheem shouted. Turning around to face him now she winked her eye at him and without warning, dropped to the floor in a hard split.

"Oh my goodness graces! Did you niggas see that? Oh my god! I said did you niggas see that?"

Nigga, if you shot the dice as much as you talk you might have won some real money by now," one of the men standing across the table from him said.

"Oh, I'ma shoot . . . I'ma shoot'em nigga."

"Watch his face when he ace," another man said.

"A hundred he four or better?" Gizmo said still trying to regain and then get ahead of his losses.

"A hundred? It's a bet!" Another man said accepting the challenge.

Raheem threw the dice from his hand and they landed on the table on the numbers four-five-six.

"I don't believe this fucking shit!" Someone exclaimed in smothered anger.

Gizmo smiled as he raked all the money to their side of the table. When he seen Raheem picking up the dice again he gave him the signal, this time Raheem dropped the dice on the table one at a time and said, "I pass the bank."

All around the table the men grunted. Gathering up all the money they'd won both Raheem and Gizmo walked over to the bar counter and ordered to drinks. They had worked out a plan before they had come there to gamble, and had given each other signals they would use to tell each other when to quit. It was the second time that the two crews had hung out together since the two crews merged, and on both occasions they had went to a gambling spot. When the barmaid brought them their drinks Raheem slid five hundred dollars across the counter to Gizmo, "Cheer up nigga, you broke even and now you're five hundred dollars ahead of the game."

"Yeah, I know," Gizmo said still maintaining a puppy dog expression, "And thanks a lot son. Your motherfucking arm was strong tonight—all them niggas is mad cause we quit, I could see it in their faces, but fuck that shit, we came here to win and we did."

"What you mean we nigga?" Raheem kidded.

"Ah nigga, you know what I mean. Now let's be outta here, I gotta go check my chick up in the Boogie down." Draining the liquor from his glass Gizmo climbed off his stool and headed for the door. Raheem, draining his glass as well, followed right behind him, calling "Yo, hey, wait up son, yo, she got a friend?"

Walking around the corner the men climbed into the Acura Legend. Gizmo, behind the steering wheel, popped in a DMX CD, and the same record that was playing in the club was now playing in the car as they drove off.

The white blip on the green screen of the lab-top sitting in Junior's lap which continued to blip and beeps constantly, was now stationary. This told him that the car he followed with his transmitter tracking device attached to the inside of its bumper had stopped. He had followed the car from East New York, Brooklyn, across the Williamsburg Bridge, onto the FDR drive, on to the Major Deegan and into the Bronx. All the while never allowing the car to get more than three miles out of his range.

Looking up from where he sat now in his car, the street signs read: Lorraine and 181st street. The people in the car he had been following were on Lorraine and 182nd street. According to the constant but stationary blip on his tracking screen, the men in the car had been stationed in one place for the last twenty minutes. He began to get curious as to what they were doing. His watch told him it was 11:45PM. He picked up his re-curve Bear bow laying on the front seat next to him and peered into the infrared scope in the direction where the Acura Legend was parked down the block. Although the tracking screen in his lap told him the car was on the right side of him, he could not see it through the scope due to all the other parked cars in back of it. The block was also congested with big oak trees on both sides of the street, making it immensely dark.

Since it wasn't twelve o'clock yet he thought it strange that he hadn't seen a single person hanging out on the streets. He decided to take a closer look in on those he sought. Closing the top of the lab top so the glow from its green screen would not illuminate inside the car he placed the re-curve bow on top. He pulled out his parking space keeping most of his attention to the right side of him where he knew they were parked as he cruised slowly down the block, though not too slow as to draw any attention.

Nearing the middle of the block the motion detector began to beep hysterically which reminded him he had forgotten to turn its volume down, but as he grew nearer he realized he needn't fear it being heard because the lyrics of 'Get at me dog,' by DMX blaring from the Acura Legend just to the right of him, over rode any other sound. When he noted that there was only one occupant in the car now he looked to both sides of him. Coming parallel with the Acura Legend he kept his head straight and his eyes looking forward.

Passing the car he made a left turn at the corner, pulled into another vacant parking space and shut off his head lights. Moving quickly now he placed his ski mask on his head rolling it up like a cap. Punched the vest on his chest a few times which reassured him from the feel of it, loaded the bow with an arrow and then placed it back into the case it came in, fastening it close. Climbing out of his car leaving its motor running which idled quietly he seen a few people walking the streets now and hoped that him being dressed in all black would not raise their suspicions. From what he could tell as he took long strides down the opposite end of the block carrying his bow in it case, no one paid him any attention.

Instead of going back the way he had come which was a shorter distance, he circled the block, once again coming from behind his prey. He stood at the corner now peering down the block at the car which still was occupied by only one person. He hugged the building on the side of him as he played the game of walking fast and then slow, closing the distance between him and those he sought. Close to ten car length away Junior drop down to one knee, opened the case on the ground, removing the bow and arrow that was already cocked. He pulled the mask down over his face . . . it was time. Rising up, he stooped over in a crouch, carrying the case in one hand and the bow in the other. He could see his mark clearly now still sitting in the passenger seat. Just then his breath caught as the dome light in the car came on, he stopped in his tracks when the car door flung open and the guy hopped out. Junior shield the bow behind its case. With nowhere to go he tried to hide himself in the darkness of the block. He was yet still outside of the guy's visual range and knew that in order for him to see him the guy would have to turn around, but just then he realized the guy had other things on his mind—it was a nature call. Pulling down his fly the guy began to piss right where he stood using the open car door as a cover. With no time to waste Junior quicken his pace now, three cars—two cars—he raised his bow—one car,—he squeezed the trigger just as the guy, shaking himself off, had turned around and looked at him. He attempted to speak while at the same time leaned backward in an effort to get out of the way. And as a result of this the arrow had lodged deep into the roof of the man's mouth entering his brain that way. His hands clawed at the arrow in his mouth before he fell to the ground. Placing the bow back in its case, Junior, squatting to the ground searched the guy's pockets while he was down there, looking for a wallet or anything that might be helpful to him in his quest, he knew it was a long shot since most criminals didn't carry a wallet.

Gizmo, coming out of the building, thought he was bugging out when he seen a black figure leaning over the body of someone on the ground. He had only been upstairs with his girlfriend for an hour and had left Raheem downstairs in the car. The music was still playing, only now the car door was open and Raheem was not in the car. Instinctively he knew that it was Raheem laying on the ground though he could not see his face, and that the guy dressed in all black was that vigilante guy they'd been talking about on the news. He thought about Raheem on the ground and cursed inwardly as he snatched the Glock from his waist. Using the music from the car to cover his sound, he rushed towards the car about six car lengths away. Yanking back the Glock's lever a bullet slid into the chamber. He intended to push this cat's wig back from close range.

In spite of the music playing loud the slick sound of lead being slammed into its fatal position, and a hammer being cocked, all together rung loudly in Junior's ears and he knew from the position he was in he was in trouble. With his back turned he contemplated how and where he would run to take cover, but just as he rose four gun shots crackled, breaking the silence in the night. The first two shots, aimed at his head had missed, but the last two he felt in his back when they pushed him forward. Spinning with the momentum of this force he turned sideways as his hand went to his waist yanking the gun free from his waist as he felt five more hot rocks when they whizzed in his direction, yet all of them had missed him except for two which caught him in the upper left shoulder which his vest did not protect. The impact of the bullets had forced him back even further and caused him to trip over the body on the ground as he released six shots from his PK19 in a sprawl position. But because the guy was a fast thinker he had taken cover in the entrance doorway of one of the building on the block. Junior kept firing at the building, only this time with slow single shots as he scrambled and climbed steady to his feet, taking quick steps backwards until he was around the corner and into his car. There hadn't been anymore return fire from the guy who shot him, but instinctively he knew he hadn't shot the guy and surmised that he must have run also.

The PK19 sat in his lap, as he drove he realized he had left the tracking device concealed inside the bumper of the Acura Legend, he also realized that right now there was nothing he could do about it. He could see the big green sign for entering the Major Deegan just a few streets away. He remembered once before how he thought he had been shot only to find out he had only been grazed, a flesh wound. But with the blood he now seen oozing down his arm, coupled with the excruciating pain he now felt in his upper shoulder, he knew he had to get back to Brooklyn, and fast.

He had to make it to Clinton Hill. There was someone there, a doctor, who for the right price would get him fixed up and also keep his mouth shut. Junior could feel his left arm as it was growing numb. I'll be alright, he told himself, make it to Clinton Hill, I'll be alright.

When Junior walked through the door of his house twenty-four hours later, the looks on both his wife and daughter's faces told him just how much they had been worried when he hadn't called or come home last night.

He'd been lucky, no bones had been broken and his arm now was in a sling. Both women jumped to their feet from the dining room chairs and rushed to him. Tears moisten Karla's eyes as she hugged him. "Ah!" Junior winced, just then Karla step back. Kim pulled the jacket from around his shoulders and they both seen the left sleeve of his shirt was missing and his arm was in a sling. They also seen the two patches of gauze taped to his shoulder, one a few centimeters below the other.

Without asking his consent Kim grabbed the black bag from his good hand that he was still reluctant to release until the look in his daughter's eyes told him she wasn't going to either. Junior's fingers then slowly released the straps of the bag and Kim placed it in the hallway closet near the front door.

Sitting him down on the couch, propping his feet up on the coffee table the women fussed over him. Because this didn't happen too often, smiling, Junior knew he was going to play it out for as long as he could.

CHAPTER SIXTEEN

The lyrics of, 'Sitting on top of the world', by Brandy and Mase, emanated from the house stereo as Junior laying flat on his back worked out on his weight bench. He grunted as 220lbs of weight on the long bar bounced up and down on his chest twenty times. Muscles on his limbs rippled as sweat dripping off his body formed a small puddle on the floor.

Since the shooting he had been working out everyday twice a day and now his shoulder was as good as new.

The only evidence to claim he had been shot were the scars he bore, for the mental ones could not be seen, but they too were there. These ones reopened each time he thought about that almost fatal night. The incident did not cripple his intentions, only delayed them. Despite of his wounds he had kept his quarries under surveillance continuously. And had even followed one of the shot-callers, who drove a Q-45 Infinity to a house upstate in Rome, New York. He was only able to ascertain that the guy was dating a white girl up there. But before he was able to learn more a strange thing had happened. Though he could not be sure, but he believed that when he looked in his rear view mirror he seen an old white man trying to take down the license plate number of his Bentley Continental. And that very next day the police from that town, hot on his trail seemed to follow him around, though he had managed to evade them it was too much of a coincidence, and he didn't believe in coincidence. Though there were no weapons in his car he knew he would have a hard time explaining away the surveillance equipment in the trunk of his car if he had gotten pulled over. Without a second thought Junior high tailed it out of that small town and came back to the city.

Justice was lying up on Riker's Island facing a gun possession charge. On the day of his arrest when Brice had gotten killed, he had heard all the shooting and had run from the bathroom and found Brice already dead. He was enraged with anger that quickly turned to fear which gripped him tightly when he looked through the restaurant plated glass window and seen a squadron of police in their cars and on feet running towards him. Lying on the bed in his cell he kicked the wall; upset because he had just returned from court and the judge had given him a hundred thousand dollar bail solely on a gun possession charge, he knew it was bullshit. The D.A. as well as the arresting officers knew that he was with the guy who had been killed, despite of Justice's claims of not have known the guy. But the statements made by the waiters in the restaurant had contradicted his story. He had tried to hide his gun in the restaurant that day when he seen the police coming but the patrons, no longer afraid, had told the authorities where he had stashed it. He knew he was still being held for questioning involving the murder and his court appointed lawyer, keeping with tradition, told him the D.A. was willing to give him a year on Riker's Island for the gun charge, providing he shed some light on the homicide case.

When Unique and Jahborn's crew had learned that it had been Blackseed who had killed Brice and that he was now dead himself, having been killed by Pataki and his men—who met up with them later claiming he had made the kill and expected to be rewarded. Or else a lot of other bodies, theirs, would be coming up missing also. The men paid him off and blew a sigh of relief. They were still on their guards however, especially after Raheem had been killed by the vigilante guy. He was still out there somewhere, free, waiting to stalk them again and take them down. Both Infinite and Unique had chided Pataki about this, telling him themselves, that it was the vigilante guy that they needed him to take care of. Pataki had informed assured them that he was going to collar the vigilante guy quicker than a rabbit gets fucked.

The men still tried to figure out what the connection was, out of the thousand of drug dealers on the street of New York City, what made him come after them in particular. They were all grateful when they received the boastful information that Gizmo had come face to face with the guy and had almost killed him, according to Gizmo. Though it was a victory, they seen it as a small one, they wanted this guy out of the picture and out of their lives for good.

Although Jahborn was upstate in Rome he had been told over the phone about Gizmo's heroic bout and had encouraged his crew to go out and celebrate.

The time was 3:30 PM when A.W. and Gizmo left Staten Island and made their way over the bridge, and back into the slums of Manhattan. They were looking for another way to carry on their celebration for what Gizmo had done to their enemy. Their Acura Legend stopped at one of the many liquor stores along the streets of Harlem. Out of the car both men entered the store where they bought a bottle of Moet and a fifth of Bacardi—dark. Making another quick stop they entered a deli and bought a lime for the liquor and a bottle of Heather's cream. On their way out they purchased a box of Dutch Master Cigars for the Hydro they had bought earlier. Back in the car Gizmo asked, "Yo. So where we're going to celebrate at yo?"

"Fuck if I know. We ain't gotta be at work for another six hours," A.W. said looking at his watch.

"So let's go chill outside in front of the spot yo, this way when we get bent off this shit we ain't gotta travel but up to the building."

"Yeah, fuck it, sounds good to me. I'm feeling you son, let's do this shit," A.W. said with little enthusiasm as he drove the car down 127ᵗʰ street. When they got there the block was crowded with people who were just hanging out. A.W. parked their car between a Ford Explorer and a Honda Civic directly beneath some trees which provided some shade from the bright shining sun.

'Sweetest thing I've ever known,' by Lauren Hill thumped loudly from the sound system of their car as they both jumped out laughing, joking, smoking trees and sipping liquor from plastic cups. The Moet, on ice in the cooler in the back seat was being saved for later. Both men teased and messed with every female they seen passing their way. After a while a Puerto Rican female named Denise, who lived in the building they hustled out of, came walking down the block towards them, and both men smiled. "Hey y'all, what's going on?" Denise said, wearing a pair of low cut white, Reebok sneakers, a red tank top and a pair of cut off jeans that dug deeply into her luscious thighs.

Gizmo, having had the hots for her had been trying to get into her draws every since they had taken over the spot.

"Ain't nothing," A.W. said, "What's going on with you?"

"Nothing," she said nicely as she leaned against their car moving up further in to the shade beneath the tree. "What's up Giz "What's up Boo—you want something to drink? Gizmo asked holding up his cup.

"What y'all drinking?"

"Bacardi—here, drink this," Gizmo said pouring more than enough liquor into his cup adding only a little Heather's cream. The day was still young and if Denise stuck around long enough he knew it would only get better.

The black of night had dropped its curtains in front of daylight. The time was 3:30AM; the streets of 127th street were practically deserted and silent.

Dressed in army fatigue Junior slid inconspicuously from his car, looking around before stepping to the back of the car. Squatting to one knee, he removed the motion detector that was still concealed inside of the bumper of the Acura Legend, which had lead him to this very specific location late yesterday. Placing the device in his pocket, he walked towards a four story tenement building that he knew the guy named Unique used as a weight house. He had learned many things about them through his surveillance and eavesdropping equipment.

This would be the last time he would use the tracking device on the Acura Legend, if, when he gained entry into the apartment and found the situation suitable to take action.

He was making his way up the second landing in the building's hallway when he heard the door of someone entering the building behind him. Thinking fast, he spun around, pulling his army cap down over his eyes and began walking back down the stairs as though he was leaving the building.

Atomic Bomb, having spoken to A.W. earlier on the phone promised to drop him off some more weed and was on his way up the stairs when he seen the tall, dark skin man in the army fatigue coming down the steps. Just then a chilling premonition overwhelmed him. Junior, recognizing the guy immediately, seen him reaching for his waist, but acting fast Junior beat him to it, drawing his weapon first.

"Yo," was the only word Atomic Bomb managed to get out before the barrel of Junior's gun was shoved viciously down his throat. To the point that he began to gag and choke as he struggled to break free of the hold the man had on him, but was slammed hard against the wall. He felt the man's strong hand relieve him of the weapon on his waist.

"One word motherfucker and you're dead! Got that?"

Atomic Bomb jerked his head up and down.

"Now we're going back upstairs together, and if you try anything, and mean absolutely anything stupid it's going to cause you to feel a pain never before known to man—you got that?" Junior shouted quietly.

With frightening, bulging eyes, Atomic Bomb jerked his head up and down again. Snatching him off the wall Junior forced him up the next flight of stairs with a gun in the back of his head.

The gun was now in a new position which poked into the ribcage of Atomic Bomb's side as he stood in front of the door knocking with a special code letting those inside know that one of their own was at the door. Knowing it was Atomic Bomb. A.W., looking through the peephole opened the door for him without a weapon. Using Atomic Bomb's body as a shield Junior forced his way into the apartment smashing A.W. against the wall. From this position of Atomic Bomb between them Junior searched A.W. for a weapon, when he didn't find one, he used both of their bodies now for a shield as he walked further into the apartment.

Gizmo, in the bathroom at this moment, not sure of the strange noise he was hearing, quickly pulled up his pants and flushed the toilet. Without bothering to wash his hands he rushed out of the bathroom and into the living room. The first thing he seen was A.W. and Atomic Bomb, but the fact that they were standing so close together bothered him causing him to frown. It was then that he seen there were too many feet. There was a third man crouching down behind them. Instinctively he knew it was the guy he had came face to face with before, though the lighting in the apartment which was dim made it difficult for him to see clearly. Gizmo dove for the guns that were in clear view on the makeshift coffee table. Taking advantage of this distraction A.W. jerked free just as Junior squeezed off two shots which splattered Gizmo's brains against the couch pillows, reaching it before Gizmo's sprawled body did. Junior let off two more shots catching A.W. in the back of his head with a force that slammed him against the wall leading out of the apartment. Knowing the report of gunfire had aroused the neighbors Junior was determine to finish what he had come there to do, "Lay down on the floor motherfucker, now! Face down!"

"Please Mr. don't kill me! You can have the money, the drugs, the guns, anything you want, just let me live Please!" Atomic Bomb pleading faced the floor with snot running down his nose. Without hesitation, Junior smashed two hot rocks into the back of Atomic Bomb's skull. This done, with his adrenaline pumping strongly throughout his body, he looked around him and seen what appeared to be the amount of two kilos of cocaine sitting on the kitchen table already in smaller, individual, plastic bags next to a stack of money. Scooping up both the money and drugs placing them in his bag he walked cautiously into the bedroom. His eyes glanced out the room's side window and he seen a squadron of silent, unmarked police cars with flashing beacons down below racing his way from several blocks over. Although he couldn't be sure but intuitively he knew that his location was their destination. And he trusted his instincts since it was the source which had kept him alive in this game.

What he didn't know was that the DEA task force, working in collaboration with two separate precincts in Manhattan had been targeting the drug house on 127th street for the last six months, and were even aware that it had been ran by someone name Blackseed but was now ran by another outfit. Having made a sufficient amount of drug purchases through undercover agents, they had intended to raid the spot one hour from now when most people would be in bed sleeping, until they had gotten a call. Standing at the window almost in disbelief, while at the same time wishing them to keep going pass the building he was in, Junior's perception of distance told him they would be there to meet him by the time he reached the bottom of the stairs. He ran towards the apartment front door as he thought of the possible ways to escape them. He thought about the roof but realized that it too was a trap since there were no buildings connected to the one he was in.

His worst case scenario was that he would have to shoot his way out, but realized the Glock in his waist along with the two other guns in the house was no match for the amount of firepower the police would mount against him. Thinking cunningly now as another thought occurred to him, he ran back toward the guns still on the table, acting fast, he scooped them up and then ran into the bathroom where he flushed all of the coke, throwing the guns into the backyard along with his bullet proof vest. Standing at the window now Junior took a deep breath as he worked up his nerves to do what had to be done. Closing his eyes tight he fired three shots; the first bullet entering the fatty tissue part of his buttocks made his legs buckle. The second and third bullet hit him in the leg and foot. Taking a deep breath, he flung the gun with all his might out of the window. Removing his gloves he threw them out into the backyard too as the first police car skidded to a stop and the men ran into the building, only Junior hadn't seen any of this. Falling to the floor he dragged himself around one of the bodies and into a corner of the living room.

He heard the police's ram as it splintered the wooded threshold of the door frame. Controlling his breathing he closed his eyes.

Over fifteen police agents entered the apartment with their guns drawn—not including the uniforms. Once they were satisfied that the apartment presented no threat lurking from any of the rooms, only then did they begin to take a body count. Although Junior could not see it he could sense the looks of horror on their faces which accompanied the tone of voice they used. He then heard someone snort, "Looks like somebody got here before we did."

"Yeah, and from the looks of it, it's probably that vigilante motherfucker." Junior then heard static come over their walkie-talkies and another voice within the house spoke into it, "I want this whole block cordon off, you guys out there got that?" There was more static and then the walkie-talkie came to life again with a metallic voice that said, "On the double chief!"

The Ghetto Soldier then heard heavy breathing of someone standing over him, and the ear shattering shout of, "THIS ONE'S ALIVE! HE'S BREATHING!" Junior felt someone feeling for a pulse in his neck and then the one in his wrist which was weakening slowly due to the amount of blood he was losing.

"Well I'll be damn."

"Well, don't just stand there dammit! Somebody radio a bus, I want this scumbag alive, he's got to tell us what happened," the chief of operation said.

"Yeah, maybe he can give you a better description of what this vigilante guy look like.

"Lucky bastard—he' the first to survive."

Because none of the officers present were black, the chief commended, "Yeah, these blacks are always the first in something."

CHAPTER SEVENTEEN

The Ghetto Soldier had been in the hospital all of a week recuperating from his self inflicted wounds. He had used a bogus name with no relatives or next of kin to contact. The police had visited him almost every day, questioning him as to what he was doing inside a noted drug house. They pumped him also, incessantly, for information on the description of the man they believed to be the vigilante, who he told them had shot him. He had accommodated them with answers that everyone reading the news paper or watching the news could have given them.

Combing the backyard the police had found his vest, all three guns and the gloves which had gunpowder residue on them. Junior thought it ironic that all of the things he had been called, he was now labeled a drug dealer. But he realized that it was a helluva lot better than being booked for a string of homicides.

On the fifth day they began to bombard him with a suspicious line of questioning, and though he had not officially been told he was being charged with anything since no drugs had been found, nor had his Miranda rights been read to him, on the sixth day his wrist had been handcuffed to the hospital bed railing. On the seventh day, the Ghetto Soldier, using a handcuff key he kept on him at all times for just such an occasion, had escaped.

*   *   *

Sitting in the comfort and privacy of his home, Unique was on the telephone in his bedroom. "Yo little brother, I'm sorry man, but our spot on one-two-seven got hit and the police shut us down. I tried calling you but your beeper was cut off and your phone just kept on ringing."

"Who was working it at the time," Jahborn asked.

"Your peeps . . . . A.W. and Giz` and even my man Atomic Bomb."

"Ah man, what's their status?" "Dead!"

The line went silent.

"I thought you said the police raided the spot? What they went out with the cops? Who did it?" Jahborn asked with hurt in his voice.

"Who else?"

"I'm on my way back now—chill."

"Oh and yo-"

"Yeah?"

"As of four weeks ago, we moved to a new spot out on Maspeth Street in Brooklyn. This one is heavily secured, and we can't be hit."

"Cool, yo did you t—"

"Yeah I took care of all the funerals."

"Yo, thanks Uiee. I'll see you when I get there."

"Don't mention it kid, what are brothers for!" Unique said and The receiver-tape recorder in the trunk of the Ghetto Soldier's car parked two blocks away from Unique's house had recorded Unique's entire conversation and automatically turned itself off when he had hung up the phone.

*   *   *

It was a rather unique three story house and impenetrable by stick up crews. Those who had tried recently had failed but never got the chance to tell others about the mistakes they had made.

The Ghetto Soldier, dressed in a Gucci outfit, walked up the porch steps leading to the house door with a diamond shape window in its center. The inside of this window was covered by a thick block of wood. Looking around him he had counted only one guy posted at the corner as a lookout man. He knocked on the door, and a few seconds later seen an eyeball appear in the peephole of the thick block of wood. He then heard the door's fortification being disengaged. When the door opened a short, stocky guy stood in the threshold. Junior was then escorted into the foyer of the house near a case of stairs. As he was being patted down with his arms raised he looked up and seen two more guys at the top of the first landing with pump shotguns resting in the bend of their arms.

The guy searching relieved Junior of the weapon concealed in the center of his back and was told it would be returned on his way back down.

When Junior reached the top of the first landing he had to make a ninety degree turn which faced another set of stairs, where at the top he seen two more men waiting with Uzi handguns in their palms. The heavy arms told him that these guys were prepared. He also noted that he hadn't seen an apartment on any of the floors he'd been on, this one included.

"Yeah dog, how much you want?" One of the guy's wearing a walkie-talkie headset said, interrupting Junior's observation.

"A big eighth." His attentions had been to sell the drugs back to them he had taken from their spot in Harlem as a ruse to get close to them, but the police had came and spoiled his plan. He also had learned from one of the cops questioning him that they had had that spot under surveillance for over six months, having heard this made him feel stupid.

He doubted though that the police knew about this place.

The guy with the headset spoke into the mike, "One coming up for a big eighth!"

Junior walked up some more steps which lead to yet another landing where he seen a steel door. Before he could knock he heard four bolt locks being slammed back and the door opened. Another man led him down a narrow corridor which lead directly into a kitchen. Through the kitchen and directly to his left he stepped into a lavishly furnished living room.

Four men were lounging around the couch and on bar stools at the counter with the butt of guns sticking out of their waist, as if for show to let anyone know that they weren't taking anything out of the place that they hadn't paid for. Junior began to have second doubts about invading this place, resigning himself to the fact that he would just have to catch these guys on the outside and pick them off one at a time as he had done with the others.

From what he could tell he did not see any way of getting at his targets in this place and survive it. It was the first time he felt a sense of despair.

One of the men sitting on the couch looked up into Junior's eyes and silently pointed at a closed door Junior had not as yet seen. Now that he did, he noted that it two was made of steel, when he knock, he heard five more dead bolts slam back before the door opened. Entering the room he seen the guy they called Hot Tee with a headset on like the guy on the staircase had on.

As Hot Tee closed the door behind him the Ghetto Soldier walked further into the room where he seen the guy name Flavor, who at the moment, sat in a swivel chair, leaning back as he filed his nails with his feet propped up against a desk. More cocaine lay atop of this desk than Junior had ever seen before at one time. Plastic bags and triple beam digital scales lay atop a small table next to the desk. The room also had an office filing cabinet, a computer screen and printer, a long leather couch, a small ice box, a microwave, a TV. and a telephone.

Hot Tee, having already heard this man's drug order before hand on his headset, already had his order ready for him in a jumbo size zip lock plastic bag,

"Count your cheese out," Flavor told the Ghetto Soldier, without moving out of his position behind the desk. Junior counted out his money and gave it to Hot Tee who then counted it out again. Satisfied, he nodded his head. Flavor then leaned over his chair, placing the package on the digital scale which read one hundred and twenty five grams.

"Take it, it's yours," he said to the Ghetto Soldier. Picking the coke up Junior took it upon himself to place it in one of the brown paper bags that were also on top of the table.

"Aw'ight Dog, come back and see us again, real soon—you heard?" Hot Tee said walking him back towards the room door. Taking notice that this room was awfully bright Junior looked up and seen that his prayers had been answered. In the center of the ceiling was a skylight made of glass. He knew now how he would penetrate this fortress as well as make his escape.

*   *   *

Dressed in all black, the Ghetto Soldier hid in the shadows of the night. He used the light from the stars to guide him over and through the debris which littered the backyard behind the weight spot he had been in earlier on Maspeth Street. Only this time he was weighed down by a very long nylon, mountain climbing rope that was coiled around his neck and under his armpit. A black heavy duty waist harness with clip hooks in the front was buckled onto his lower body. Two hard acrylic plastic wheels, five by ten inches in diameter, better known as a pulley, were slung over his back.

Junior Washington scaled the wall at the back of the weight house with the agility of a cat burglar. Reaching the roof he moved about noiselessly, with the light feet of a pigeon. He snailed his way over to the house skylight and peeked into the room down below. It was dark except for a bluish glow he knew was coming from either the computer screen or TV. Satisfied with this, he backed away from the skylight and began to remove his equipment and sat up his apparatus. Carefully, he lightly placed his rope of the roof floor. Sucking in his breath he then removed a wide, thin, but sturdy piece of plywood from beneath his vest. It would be what he would stand on to minimize the cuts he would sustain when he dropped down through the glass skylight. Holes had been drilled into the wood and laced with strings for his feet to slide under and into. He tied one end of the rope around the chimney before threading it through the harness around his waist. He then lined the ropes up on the wheel tracks and pulled it until it became taut. This done, he tied the second end of the rope around the chimney wall as well. Back at the skylight he stepped on the plywood inserting his feet into the strings. He pulled one of the Calico's from the holster strapped to his thigh. He was ready now. He leaned over and peeked down into the skylight one final time. Taking a deep breath, he leaped into the air, when he re-conformed to gravity, glass shattered everywhere beneath the weight of his body crashing down, down, and down.

The moment the rope went taut and gave his body a shattering jilt, his finger greedily sucked on the trigger of the Calico in his hand. Suspended in mid air, dangling from a string, he caught both men, Flavor and Hot Tee off guard, who at the moment were still scurrying away from the falling glass that was coming down in large jagged edges. Both men ran to the filing cabinet frantically trying to open it, but the hot rocks spitting from the Calico in the Ghetto Soldier's hand, which had a strong desire for food of the flesh, ate into them, causing their body motions to move as though they were puppets on strings, before falling to the floor grotesquely disfigured.

When Junior realized that everyone in the room was dead he released his finger from the trigger stopping the deadly spray from the Calico. At this time there were holes in the walls all around the room. Cotton from the pillows on the couch floated in the air around the room. Junior, still dangling from the rope in mid air, spun around and around the room taking survey. His entry from the ceiling had triggered an alarm that had been attached to the skylight, and was now ringing loudly throughout the house. Unclipping his harness he dropped a few feet down on top of the desk where the cocaine still laid. He snatched up four stacks of money that was lying out on the table quickly placing them into the black sack dangling beneath his arm. All the while listening to the men banging on the other side of the door trying to get in. He ran over to the filing cabinet, looked inside and seen two handguns and four boxes of bullets. Snatching them out, he placed them in the microwave and set the timer for three hours. He then climbed back on top of the desk, refastened the rope to the harness and used the pulley to roll himself back up to the roof. On the roof, he left the equipment where it was and made his getaway.

CHAPTER EIGHTEEN

Infinite and his woman Asia were sitting on a cream color leather sofa in their living room while listening to an Isley Brothers CD, and at the same time looking at themselves on a fifty-six inch screen TV. Using a camcorder they had filmed themselves during one of their hot and sticky sexual episodes that had been so hot it had left the camera lens steamed up.

On top of the fifty-six inch TV. sat a thirteen inch color TV. with a blue ribbon wrapped around it. It was a gift that Infinite had given to his woman C'Asia. At this moment this TV. too was on with its volume turned off.

One of the things C'Asia appreciated about her man was that he never brought any of the problems he had out in the streets home, because home was where he unwind and devoted his time to her.

In the privacy of their home Infinite was stripped down to his boxer shorts and C'Asia wore nothing but a burgundy gee-string and matching bra. Two glasses and a chilled bottle of Crystol sat on the cocktail table. A pound of weed lay out in the open on the seat of a wooded back chair next to the table. The weed was Infinite's personal stash. He had been bagging it up before C'Asia had suggested that they watch the tape. Just recently he had concluded that he was consuming too much weed. Bagging it up was the only way for him to monitor how much he was smoking, this way he limited himself to only seven bags a day now. Before this, he use to run through a pound of weed in a matter of three weeks.

Leaning forward now with his full attention on the screen Infinite exclaimed, "Pla-dow! You see that? Do you see that? I'm tearing that pussy up—ooo! Look at your face! Look at your face! You was feeling it," he said leaning over grabbing C'Asia who at the moment was sitting next to him smiling, and embarrassed. She remembered the scene from this tape well, it was one of the few times that she had been exceedingly horny and one of the less than few times she had let herself go completely. She couldn't be sure but she believed that the fact that they were filming it had a lot to do with it, which also had been the first time. At the moment she felt strange, exposed, seeing herself on the screen, doing things that even now made her blush, surprisingly, she was also getting horny again from watching it.

"My Ill-nana was just hungry for her chocolate bar daddy . . . . What can I say," C'Asia said leaning over and caressed him while her eyes stayed glued to the screen.

Without warning Infinite jumped up from the couch, walked over to the sound system, took the Isley Brothers and replaced it with "Too Close," by the group called Next.

"You know what I want you to do for me boo?" he said walking back towards her. He placed the weed that was in the chair on the floor.

"What's that daddy?" C'Asia said, giggling, feeling a little tipsy from the bottle of Crystol they had already consumed and the second one they were now working on.

"I want you to dance for me real sexy like—real nasty like—real freaky like. Would you do that for me baby?" He asked sitting back down.

"You mean you want to dance like a stripper? You want me to be a slut?" she asked accusingly, and then to his surprise, she said, "okay." Taking a drink from her glass she stood up moving her body slowly to the music as if getting a feel for it. Looking at him she said, "I'ma dance like them hoes' do in them clubs you be going to." Setting her glass down C'Asia began to get seriously involved into the music. Swaying her hips provocatively from side to side. Getting an idea, she stopped, ran to the closet near the hall and put on a pair of four inch spike heels, and came back. The four inch heels now made her ass arch out even more, making it seem bigger than what it actually was.

Her body swayed to the music again in front of Infinite who sat now with lust in his eyes. She turned her back to him giving him an ass shot and began doing a dance Jamaican women were known for doing. She then made her ass cheeks jiggle as she put her hands behind her removing her bra. It dropped to the floor and she kicked it to the side. With her back still to him she spread her legs, leaned down forward and touched her toes. Shaking her ass this way, she looked at him from between her legs seeing how much it was really turning him on. Standing up straight again she turned around to face him and began to grind the lower part of her body hard and seductively. Sitting back in the wooded back chair, speechless, Infinite flogged his flag pole that stood erect in the air. C'Asia decided now to give him a lap dance, she walked towards him, "Honey, you still haven't told me why you gave me the little TV. wrapped in that blue ribbon?" Straddling his lap now she said, "It ain't Valentine's Day, and it ain't my birthday so what's it really for Infinite?"

He had told her that he bought the TV. for her solely because she had a sweet ass. In truth, it was a gift he had received from finger hut, with a note telling him he had won a prize. Although he didn't know what the hell they were talking about, and that they had made a mistake, he wasn't about to tell them or give it back. So instead he had told C'Asia that he bought it for her.

"Like I told you boo, I bought it for you because your ass is the bomb! You got the bomb ass! And that's why the TV. is wrapped in ribbons, cause you got the first prize blue ribbon ass baby!"

C'Asia giggled as he pulled her Gee-string to one side. Her hands then reached down, inside of his shorts and gripped him, "UUm!" she crooned, "You're the man of steel daddy," she said guiding him into the softest place on earth. Wrapping her legs around the back of the chair now she began a slow grind while sitting on his lap. The better the feeling got the harder their breathing came. After a short while C'Asia found herself bouncing up and down in a thrall of ecstasy. Just then the telephone began to ring on the night table beside them. Without breaking his momentum Infinite reached over and snatched it off the hook, "Peace!"

"Peace God," Unique said on the other end, "I can't talk long God, I'm just calling to remind you of the meet we got tomorrow night with that jive ass devil." Unique said referring to the cop Pataki.

"Ye, yea, yeah God I knoaaa . . . . remember."

"What the fuck . . . what the fuck you doing?" Unique said and then grew silent. He heard the music in the background playing and the unmistakable voice of C'Asia who was grunting and speaking in syllable tones.

Unique laughed, "You fucking God—ain't you?"

"Why . . . why-equal-self, God."

"Well listen," Unique chuckled, I'm not gonna hold you up, Jahborn is suppose to meet us there too. We're gonna double what we have been giving Pataki, but he's really gonna have to do something about this vigilante motherfucker yo."

"Uum . . . Ah, uh, no doubt, no doubt, true indeed God.

And uh . . . . we also gotta find another spot."

"Yeah. Listen, I'ma let you get back to your business—peace out."

"Peace!" Infinite replied, dropping the phone.

The resonant chamber located in the portable color TV. in Infinite's living room acted as a diaphragm that responded to every sound made in the area of the house. The tape recorder in the van parked a block away automatically turned itself off.

CHAPTER NINETEEN

Donald Pataki, his wife Gloria and their son Donald Jr. lived in a three bedroom house on 87th street in Howard Beach. They had been residents of this area all of their lives. They had seven more years of mortgage payments before they could own the house, but thanks to Donald's many different ways he found to supplement their income and the salary he made as a veteran police officer, their mortgage of seven years, would now be paid ahead of time in two weeks, making them proud and complete owners of their home.

Gloria and Donald had known each other practically all their lives. Having grew up together in the same neighborhood, attended the same schools, they became childhood sweethearts married fifteen years ago when they learned she was pregnant with Donald Jr.

Like all newlywed couples, at the beginning of their relationship, their nights had been filled with lusty, hot, steamy passion. And they couldn't seem to keep their hands off of each other. And when Donald had quit his job as a store clerk and joined the police force, Gloria knew then that her future would be secured. She remembered how they use to go out regularly and visit their in-laws almost every weekend. Photos of them as a couple graced the walls of the homes of both of their relatives. But as the years passed by the passion slowed down and the couple began to settle in. She had no illusion about this and had figured as much, knowing that one day the novelty of them being together would dissipate and that they would just shift to the second phase of marriage. So at those times when they were out in public and she noticed how certain other women would catch Donald's eye, Gloria paid it no mind.

She had even suspected that her Donald fooled around, but since he never disrespected her she pretended not to know. As far as she was concerned, he was just sowing what little oats he still had left, and that it too would pass soon. There was no doubt in her mind that Donald still loved her but she knew he was also still in love with her. The things he still did to her behind the closed doors of their bedroom made her blush each time she thought about it.

However, within the last few years Gloria pensively recognized that there was another shift in their marriage and another side to Donald she had never seen before. He began to display mood swings and he drank more now than ever before to the point of becoming a slush. He kept later hours than he use to and sometime didn't come home at all or call. Over the last eight months he had even become violent and abusive towards her and their son. Gloria attributed it to the work he did out in the streets, and that it was getting to him. She had told him that no one could be exposed to evil and degraded elements out there in the streets over a long period of years and escape being affected by it themselves. And though he had never seemed able to tie the two together, Gloria knew it was the niggas he chased behind and locked up every day and their debased nature that was rubbing off on her Donald. She remembered the stories that he use to tell her when asked about his day at work. She knew how Donald felt about niggas, feeling the same way was just another thing they had in common. And that's why, when he came home from work, she treated him like a king, pampered him and catered to his every whim.

*   *   *

Ignat stood five feet five inches tall, she had shoulder length black hair, a very light skin complexion and green eyes. With a nearly nonexistent waist she had a knockout body for her size. And was aware of the affect it had over the men who tried constantly to get into her tight, form fitting jeans. Most of the men who knew her for her trade often referred to her as the Green Eyes Bandit. Her hustling skills had allowed her to be an independent woman; it was the thing that also gave her the cutting edge when it came to the exchange of give and take with men. Since she did not depend on any of them for anything but sex it enabled her to be the one who picked and chose instead of it being the other way around. That is, until Pataki came around, and that changed everything.

Now every time a man tried to get next to her Pataki would chase him off by scaring him away.

Many of the nights she wished fate had never sent him her way. She had come to learn that he was a psychopath with a license to kill. He was the first man to have ever hit her, and also the first who had ever really frighten her. There had been times when she thought she had him under her spell as she placed so many other men, but it had been at those times that she learned, and learned the hard way that he wasn't under her spell but that she was under his. He was in control. And though she had never been a prostitute, Pataki's mood swings gave her a general idea of what having a pimp was probably like; she had read many black urban books and could identify him with the characters of pimps. The way he would be sweet and gentle with her and then without even a moments warning turn into a stark raving maniac. She observed that the only person who seemed to have the slightest control over him was her daughter Princess. But the thoughts of her daughter being with her when he was around frighten her. For all she knew, he was grooming her to one day become his mistress too.

There were also times when she could have sworn he did not see her as being black; sometimes she thought it had a lot to do with her lily white skin. He would talk to her at times about black people in a negative and totally disrespectful way, as if he didn't know she was black. But then there were those other times when he would not let her forget what she was—not that she tried too. Proud of her heritage, she would sometimes seize with anger silently as she listened to him talk. She bid her time as she thought of ways of getting rid of him without running the risk of him setting her up to go to jail as he often threaten her he would.

Being his mistress, she was grateful for the fact that he was married and still had a wife, because she knew she could not take seeing him every day. And the thought of him moving in with her was a nightmare which made her skin crawl. She had once been arrested after meeting him, for shop lifting and he had gotten her off of it scot free. She didn't know whether to be happy or sad since she knew it would put her further into his debt. She had even fault hard against him helping her to pay her rent, but he had insisted and she knew better than to get him upset. One night after having forced sex with him the germ of an idea occurred to her when he had told her his wife and son were going over to her mother's for a week. It was then she planted the seed in his head, telling him she wanted to make love to him in the bed he shared with his wife because the thought of it was such a turn on. Her plans were to leave her panties or some lipstick in the house where his wife could find them, when she came back home. Which then would be just enough to make her suspicious of him, and maybe then their arguments would be enough to make him stay home and out of her bed. She had even thought about disguising her voice and calling his wife, but something told her he would figure out it was her and a mistake like that would cost her. But leaving her panties or some lipstick, anyone could make that kind of mistake.

When she first had insinuated this idea to Donald he had called her a dumb black nigga bitch, and that he would put his foot up her ass if she didn't pipe down. But at the risk of getting beat up she persisted, knowing that he was a daring person and would soon warm to the thrill of the idea. She knew he liked living on the edge and could sense when he felt the charge of the challenge of being able to pull something like that off. She knew it was getting away with it part that excited him most, and made him agree to do it.

Pataki's house was located on a dead end block which prevented probing eyes from prying in. In fact, he knew that his neighbors would have to become suspicious looking in order to be nosy. The day his son and wife left for her mother's, Pataki arrived at Ignat's house at two o'clock in the morning to get her. But using her body and her charm, she had talked him out of it and they stayed at her place for five more days. When it was a day before his wife was to return Ignat tried, but could put him off no longer. It was his idea now and he had persisted that they do it before his wife returned tomorrow.

Packing an extra lipstick and a pair of panties in her purse, Ignat allowed him to take her to his house in Howard Beach. Her spirits had been dampening because she knew they had too much time before his wife would return. Thinking back, she later realized that subconsciously, she really wanted them to get busted by his wife, but time was not on her side, or so she thought.

Ignat was sprawled out on Pataki's wife bed performing oral sex on him when she felt a cold draft of wind blowing across her ass cheeks that was protruding in the air. Since the bedroom door had been closed she nor had he heard anyone coming up the carpet stairs.

Pataki, at the time, enthralled in ecstasy by Ignat's performance, had his eyes closed, while listening to "Lucy in the sky", blasting from the speaker of the alarm clock radio he had won in a contest, had not heard Gloria's car when it had drove up into the driveway. And still didn't have a clue that something was wrong until Ignat stopped what she was doing which then caused him to open his eyes. When he looked up he saw Gloria standing in the doorway with an ashen face. Her trembling hand covered her scream from her mouth. Angered, hurt, betrayed, Gloria fought back the bile which tried to rush out of her throat. When it registered to Pataki that what he was seeing was not an illusion and that it was really his wife Gloria standing in the door's threshold, his erect flag pole began to fly now at almost half mast and he kicked Ignat in the face in an effort to get from beneath her and out of the bed. Just then Gloria, crying, rushed out of the room and stomped down the steps. Pataki could hear her screaming, shouting and throwing things around downstairs in the kitchen.

"Shit! . . . Christ! She came back sooner than she was suppose to," Pataki shouted as he got dressed indulging in self-talk. Suddenly he looked up and seen Ignat standing there in the nude, as if seeing her for the first time, he yelled, "What the hell you're just standing there for, bitch! Get dressed before you find yourself on the streets naked and then I'll have to arrest you for indecent exposure! Shit!" he barked again, and then rushed out of the room and down the stairs behind Gloria. Ignat smiled when he left the room, jumped in the air with glee and clapped her hands.

When she got dressed she made her way down the stairs of Pataki's house and seen him in the kitchen doing a cross between dodging the kitchen knife Gloria was swinging at him and trying to hug her to him for comfort and to calm her down.

"Honey . . . honey, listen to me . . . I know what this looks like . . . but I can explain . . . I . . ." Pataki backed away from his wife who was preparing to launch at him with the knife in her hand. Seeing Ignat, he hissed, Get Outta Here . . . Wait For M e Outside."

"YOU BASTARD!" Gloria cried. "Wait for you outside?" she shouted, enraged, not believing he could ever want to see the woman again. As Ignat made her way towards the house front door she seen Pataki trying to win over his son, "Listen to me son, I know that y—," but Donald Jr. pulled away from him and said, "How could you dad?" . . . . And with a nigga!"

CHAPTER TWENTY

Justice was grateful for the job he had gotten on Riker's Island as a suicide watchman. His duty was to walk up and down the hallway and monitor the other inmates in their cells to make sure none of them tried to kill themselves by hanging up or cutting their wrist. For this job Justice was paid twenty-five dollars a week. Outside of the cook position in K.K., which was the cafeteria where the correction officers ate at, the suicide position was the highest paying job for an inmate. One of the fringe benefits of this job during the graveyard shift was that he was allowed to use the phone late at night and for as long as he liked.

Monica had no idea that the nice looking man she had let into the house last month posing as an electrician for the housing department was not a housing department worker at all. The tall good looking guy had changed at least two of the electric socket outlets in the house that she had been told were defective—she didn't see anything wrong with that.

*   *   *

Both of Jahborn's hands gripped the steering wheel tight as he drove through the streets at three o'clock in the morning like a mad man. The falling rain had made the streets slippery. A few miles back a car had almost side swiped Jahborn's car as a result of him having ran a red light. It was Friday night, early Saturday morning, and he had just left the club Bentley's where, he had run into the guy name Cory who he had been looking for some time ago for giving Monica a hard time and trying to feel her ass. But what had started out as a confrontation with him had turned into a shocking, eye opening revelation.

The guy Cory had told him all about Monica, his Monica who had been creeping with another guy name Justice who worked for his brother Unique. At first Jahborn had thought Cory was just reaching for straws to get around the tall can of ass whipping he had coming. But Cory had undisputable facts of information, all the dirt, as well as other people who happened to be in the club at the time to verify Cory's story. Cory even knew that the guy Justice was now locked up on Riker's Island, and had seen Monica on several occasions in the visiting room with him while he had been visiting one of his friends.

Cory had dates, times, and places; he even knew about Monica's birthmark, which was the shape and size of a baby fish and located only centimeters away from her vagina. Boasting and bragging, Justice had told Cory's man all about his and Monica's freaky episodes when he was out there.

Jahborn had to face the fact that what he heard was true, and now he was fuming. In his vision all he could see was white rage, as thoughts, like bombs, exploded on contact in the minefield inside his head. He wanted to know why? How long had it been going on? Cory had also reminded him of the time that he and his three friends had come to the house months ago looking for him, only he hadn't been home. How that had been the first time he had seen the guy Justice going into the building with Monica. This information made Jahborn feel real suckerish, like a sucker for love as he thought about the lame shit Monica had told him that day she had tried to cover her tracks by putting it all on Cory and his friends.

Jahborn had seen the guy Justice on two occasions, because he was a nobody he hadn't paid him much attention on either occasions. Now he found himself trying to place his face, but on the screen of his mind he could get the contours of an image. Tonight marked the fourth night he was back from Rome, New York. He had plans to meet up with his brother

Unique and Infinite tomorrow night at club ESSO's. He knew he had an image and a status to protect and hold up, but when he met with his brother he intended to find out as much as he could about the guy Justice without revealing the real reasons why he wanted to know. At the moment he wanted to know where the guy lived? Since he was presently in jail Jahborn wanted to go after his family, to hurt them, shoot them and keep shooting them until his gun ran out of bullets as he knew his man Gizmo, god bless the dead—would do if he was still alive. But the vigilante guy had ruined that. Jahborn wished the vigilante was around now, the way he felt, he knew he would bite the guy's nose off his face and rip his anatomy apart with his bare hands. Right now he was in the mood to kill and would do just that to anyone who stood in his way at the moment.

He pities the police if they stopped him now, he had questions he needed answers to, and was determined to let nothing stop him until he got them. The fact that he now knew Monica had fucked another man was driving him crazy in the head; it also made him feel inadequate. He wanted to know what the guy Justice had that he didn't? What had he done wrong to make her turn to another man in the first place? A low life worker at that. He wanted to know how many times they'd fucked? And why would she let Justice do it to her? How did they meet, and where at?

He was only a few minutes away from home now but couldn't get there soon enough. He burrowed himself down further in deep thought. Did she suck his dick? And if so, she had the nerves to come home and kiss me afterwards like nothing happened, "THE BITCH!" He shouted within his car. He thought back to all the times it could have happened, all those times he wasn't around. He thought back to all those times he had tried to persuade her into letting him fuck her in the ass, only she kept putting him off, whining about how she was scared and knew it was going to hurt. He wondered now if it was all a come on. Did she let Justice fuck her in the ass? From personal experience he knew that people who cheated usually performed in sexual acts that they wouldn't do with their real mates. With this in mind he began to visualize Monica laying down getting fucked in the ass by Justice, from her doggy style position he seen her looking back enthralled, wearing the same horny, facial expression he himself had seen her make.

The sight of this enraged him even more and he began to feel sick at the stomach. Nauseated, he forced back the sour, bitter, bile taste which tried to force itself up from his throat. The tears falling from his eyes now blurred his vision as he screamed, "After everything I done for you—how could you do this to me you BITCH!" Just then he heard the scraping sound of metal rubbing up against metal and realized it was his car rubbing up against parked cars, quickly, he swerved back into the middle of the street before any further damage could be done. If he had hit someone right now by mistake he wouldn't stop, he had to get home to Monica, his Monica, the Monica who had betrayed him for another man. As pretty as she was he now knew she was nothing but a whore, slut and an ungrateful bitch.

Jumping out of his car Jahborn had no idea he had been followed, followed since he left the club in Manhattan. In his emotional state and urgency, he hadn't even parked his car right and its rare end protruded out in the street. With the weather being what it was, made it an accident just waiting to happen. Somewhere in some part of his brain he realized this but it didn't matter, he was now in the zone and the zone was a place where nothing much mattered. Jahborn made his way into his building.

As he exit the elevator making his way down the hall he could hear the lyrics of "My little secret", by the group Escape playing low on the radio in the kitchen inside the apartment, as well as the telephone ringing, and wondered briefly who the hell would be calling his house at this hour. When he got into the house the phone had already stop ringing. As he made his way up the stairs within the house he could hear Monica's voice, she was speaking in low tones. When he stepped into the bedroom she was lying on top of the bed wearing a pink teddy with black lace and hadn't heard him come in. Upon seeing him the smile on her face vanished and she quickly hung up the phone. Seeing the expression on his face she immediately became solicitous, asking as she sat up, "What's the matter Jah?—what's wrong?

Jahborn rushed towards the bed, shouting, "What's wrong?" You're what's wrong bitch!" Before Monica could react she felt the vicious blow connecting with the side of her face jarring her balance. Frighten out of her wits Monica grabbed her face and scurried towards the head of the bed. Somewhere in her mind she knew she had been hit but she didn't know if she had been slapped or punched. "Whoa . . . . What I do daddy? Why are you beating on me? You ain't never hit me before daddy. What I do daddy? What I do?" Monica cried.

"Who the fuck was you just talking to on the phone?" Monica looked over at the phone as she thought, "I—I—" she stammered, "I was talking to Tanya," she spat out quickly, thinking straight now. The woman Tanya she referred to was her girlfriend who knew lived five floors below them.

"Tanya huh?" As he rushed to the phone Monica scrambled even further away from him out of fear. He looked like he was high off of something she had never seen him use before.

"I know all about you and your nigga bitch," he said now pressing star sixty-nine, "and unless you come clean bitch you and that nigga both are dead."

"Nigga? What nigga, daddy?" She said in a tone of voice indicating that she found it ludicrous that he would even think such a thing about her. "Jahborn I don't mess with nobody, nobody daddy—just you!" Monica began to cry.

The phone on the other end of the line began to ring in Jahborn's ear, and suddenly when he didn't hear it ring anymore he spoke, "Hello"

Seconds later he heard a computerize musical tone and then a recorded message: 'I'm sorry, but this is a restricted phone and no calls permitted to go through.'

"What she saying Daddy?" Monica asked, stalling for time, knowing that she hadn't been speaking to her girlfriend Tanya, but Justice. Jahborn slammed the phone down, pressing star sixty-nine he tried again. When the recording came on again it made him even tighter. He began talking to the recording as if it would somehow allow Justice to hear him speak. "Yeah Justice I know it was you motherfucker, I just want you to know that I'ma kill you nigga—your whole fucking family nigga—word is bond. You and this bitch here is dead." Upon hearing him say the name Justice, Monica's heart dropped.

Without warning he threw the phone at her with all his might, she ducked, and a good thing she did, upon impact against the wall the phone scattered into many pieces. "You say you was talking to Tanya, I say you're lying bitch, you been a liar all the while, I just didn't know it." He said snatching her by the back of her neck, dragging her from the bed. Monica struggled to keep up as he pushed her through the house and out of the door.

"Where . . . where we going?"

"You said you was talking to Tanya right bitch? So she can't be asleep that fast. I want her to tell me that she just got off the phone with you. And if you say one word to her while I'm speaking I'm gonna stick my shit up your pussy and empty the clip out bitch," Jahborn hissed. For some reason he felt that if he could prove that she was lying now, it would add that last bit of proof he needed to cause her serious bodily harm.

Monica stalled, "It's late Jahborn, and we can't be knocking on her mother's door at this hour."

This comment caused her to get slapped again. "Shut up bitch and move."

"But I ain't got no clothes on Jahborn. You got me out here in this hallway with no clothes on. I can't believe you're doing this to me, don't do me like this Jahborn!"

"Bitch when you're dead you don't need clothes!"

She had been forced down the stairs with nothing on but her teddy.

Jahborn knocked on the door of apartment 17H, while Monica, standing a few feet away faced the wall so she could not be seen or give her friend any warning.

Jahborn knocked harder on the door the second time. Several seconds later he seen the peephole move and then heard the voice of an old woman, "What do you want Jahborn?"

"I'm sorry to wake you Ms. Johnson but I need to speak to Tanya, it's about Monica and it's an emergency." Upon hearing this the lady Ms. Johnson open her door, and said, "Come on in."

"No-no, thank you Ms. Johnson but I'll wait right here. And again I'm sorry to wake you but Monica ain't home and she didn't leave a note," Jahborn was making it up as he went along, "And I'm worried about her."

"Well I hope the poor girl is alright. Wait right here, I'll go wake up my daughter." While she left to get her daughter Jahborn looked over at Monica whose legs were now trembling as she stood facing the wall in her teddy.

When Tanya came to the door several seconds later Jahborn said, "Yo what's up Tanya? I'm sorry to be waking you up yo' but Monica ain't home and she ain't leave a note or nothing and this shit got me worried sick about her." his facial expression matched his words, "Do you know where she's at? Have you seen or spoke with her today?"

Tanya grew silent for a second, she knew about the affair Monica was having but the guy was in jail now. So she could not think of any place else that Monica would be other than home. She began to worry herself. "I spoke to her earlier today."

"When? . . . . what time was that?"

"That was real early today during a commercial when we was watching Jerry Springer."

"That's all, that's the only time? Not tonight?"

"No, just that one time," Tanya said, "did something happen Jahborn?" She asked, feeling that he was acting a bit strange.

"What you mean? . . . . Something like what?"

"I don't know—a fight maybe? It's just not like Monica to go somewhere and not tell nobody."

"Well, I'm going to find her, in fact, when I get back upstairs I'm going to call her mom's crib. Thanks anyway Tanya," he said walking away.

"Tell her to call me when you find her Jahborn."

"Aw'ight," he said and then heard her door close. At this moment he felt as if he was on an emotional roller coaster ride. Monica was truly scared now; he could see it in her eyes that were now pleading. For some reason, in her frighten emotional and mental state, she looked to him more beautiful and sensual than he'd ever recall seeing her look before. He was happy now, he had the last shred of proof he needed.

Grabbing her roughly again behind the neck he forced her up the hallway stairs. His emotions at this moment were going back and forth each time their bodies made contact. It seems that this incident had made more senses more acute, and her skin, her body seemed so much softer now. He knew he still wanted her. The ice in his heart seemed to melt just a little. He knew that she knew the jig was up and she was scared, but he also knew that the moment she hesitated in answering any of his questions he was going to try and mold his fist into her face. His spirits lifted a little, he felt better and could see clearer now.

As they reached the landing to their floor Monica broke down, "I'm sorry Jahborn, I swear I'm sorry daddy. I know I was wrong. I'll tell you whatever you want to know. Everything you wonna know. Just please don't hate mmmeeee! She cried.

"I won't boo," he lied, "just tell me the truth and we can talk about this like adults."

"You can beat me Jahborn, I don't care, I know I was wrong but just please don't hate me, don't leave me daddy!" She said wiping the mucus running from her nose. "I love you Jahborn, I swear I do!"

Now that his vision was clear, as they entered the house he got a mental flash of himself jumping out of the car before coming upstairs. And not only did he realize he didn't park the car right, he realize he had left the keys in the ignition. He spoke out loud, "Listen I want you to go inside right now."

"Bu..but I thought you said we was going to talk?"

"We are, but for now I want you to think about everything you have to tell me. But its gotta be the truth, and you can't leave

159

nothing out or I'ma hit you and I don't wonna do that, but I gotta know everything, starting from how y'all met?"

"We met in the M—."

"Sshhh, not now, when I come back, right now I gotta go downstairs and get something outta the car."

"I hope you are not going to go get a gun Jahborn?"

In answering her question he pulled his gun off of his waist and placed it on the kitchen table. He felt that this should convince her plenty. "If I wanted to shoot you I could have been shot you. We gonna talk, I need you to help me understand this . . . this shit." He rushed out of the apartment.

*　*　*

Junior snatched the headphones off his ears when he seen Jahborn rushing out of the building. He had been listening to Monica talking to her girlfriend on the phone the moment Jahborn had left the apartment. He heard her tell her girlfriend everything that happened. Her girlfriend had asked if she wanted her to call the police for her but after hesitating for a second, declined. On second thought told her if she didn't call back in an hour to call them.

Junior's car at this moment was on the opposite side of the street, facing the opposite direction of Jahborn's car. Junior picked up the Halfner-Schnit Compound bow with the night star scope on the seat next to him and looked into the scope. He saw Jahborn jogging down the walkway towards his car. Junior's left hand finger depressed the button making his window roll down.

Jahborn looked through the car window on the passenger side and seen the keys still in the ignition.

Junior pressed the button on the bow and the wench began to crank back the bow's bridge track.

As Jahborn reached the driver's side of his car he slipped on the wet asphalt.

Junior squeezed the trigger and 350lbs of pressure released. The arrow, like a scud heat seeking missile hit its target, catching Jahborn in the left side of the chest as he was getting up from the ground.

The arrow, piercing his heart, exited out of his back and entered the car's door on the driver's side, exit the passenger side door, and implanted itself deep into the bark of a tree with a thump.

Jahborn grabbed the place on his chest where his heart use to be before, looking down at it his face showed disbelief as he slid to the ground with his back against the car door.

Junior, placing the bow back on the seat next to him rolled his window back up and then drove off.

CHAPTER TWENTY-ONE

It was now two weeks later. Late Saturday night, early Sunday morning. Pataki was sitting in the VIP section of club ESSO'S. He knew that this was the hour that the Jungle Bunnies came out to hop around and shake their asses. To him it was the only thing they did well, since he felt they were too ignorant, lazy or both to do anything else. He believe they were just a waste of matter taking up valuable space on the earth. Mention the word work to any of them and they would try to run from America back to Africa to get away from you. They were a bunch of good for nothing whose only interest seemed to be in killing and selling drugs to one another, which to him were the same thing. Fucking and making babies that they left for welfare to take care of.

The fact that he had spent more time and bought more clothes for his mistress daughter than her own father did was proof enough for him that this was true.

He also believed that Blacks were a gift from God given to white people, especially to him to govern. It was why he had become a cop. He knew he would have the legal rights to beat the shit out of them and keep them in line. He had proof that they were unorganized, stupid, cowards and dumb. He believed that a good example of making his point were the two assholes sitting across the table from him. They had the nerve to even call themselves God, and told him that he was the Devil. He felt that if what they believed was true . . . well then the devil was kicking God's ass and he was truly stupid for not trying to do anything to change it around. He had made them show him their lessons a long time ago. And what he had read made him laugh.

Pataki had learned long ago before he made Detective rank that to get ahead in his field of business a person had to be ambitious. One had to get as close to the action as he could. He knew that it wasn't the guys in the squad cars who got the scoop, but the cops who walked the streets of the jungle. Because only through integrating the jungle would one get to know that jungle and the natives in it. And that was what he did. So as far as he was concern, he was Tarzan.

At the moment he stared at the two guys across the table, one called himself Unique and the other, himself Infinite. Only he didn't see anything Unique about them aside from the fact that he found them both infinitely stupid. Pataki knew that Julius Caesar, the great ruler of the Roman Empire had the right idea when he coin the phrase: 'I Came, I Saw and I Conquered.' Pataki knew that he probably had blacks in mind when he said this. Only they were called moors' at that time. Well since then Pataki had coin he own phrase which went: 'Imprison their men, brain wash their children, and rape their women.'

At the moment the two guys before him owed him some money and he was here to collect and straighten some things out. Their last two payments were less than what they should have been. On both occasions they had been bitching about Blackseed, another smuck he was extorting, they claim was stopping his cash flow. Now Blackseed was dead they were trying to put it on another guy who stayed in the news as the vigilante. Everyone was looking to nail this guy, especially him. But liking the idea of seeing them shook, he wasn't, until now, in a hurry to see it as a pressing matter. "Ah, keep the change," Pataki told the waiter with the phat ass placing his seventh drink for the night in front of him. He knew he could afford to be generous since these smucks were paying the tab. Infinite had ordered him a Thug Passion. Because it had a kick to it Pataki liked it, until he learned it had been named by the late rap artist Tupac Shakur. Pataki pushed the drink to the side refusing to finish it. "So did you niggas get a make on this other guy yet?"

"Naw," Infinite replied, "nothing other than what's already on the news."

"Yeah and if it's this guy y'all had, y'all let him go, cause he wasn't one of our boys," Unique added.

"Any idea why they call him the Vapor?" Pataki asked.

"Cause after he gets busy he always manages to disappear into thin air.

Pataki thought for a moment about all the publicity he would get if he caught this guy. Infinite bought him out of his reverie, "Since nobody ever seen this guy he could walk right next to anyone and they wouldn't know it was him."

Pataki smiled, "Yeah, and you niggas forgot to mention the hard on he's got for drug dealers." Laughing, Pataki slapped Infinite on the shoulder. Turning serious again he leaned forward, "You guys got something for me?

"Yeah," Infinite passed him an envelope beneath the table. They considered it rock-A-bye money. Before Pataki could speak Unique did, "Not only is it the full amount, there's extra. If you'd like it to stay that way find this guy and get him out of our hair."

Pataki felt the weight of the envelope. Sliding it into his pocket he stood up and drained his glass. "Well I'm outta here, I gotta date."

Both men knew it was with Ignat.

"But don't worry, this vigilante, Ghetto soldier nigga, is as good as got, use just keep this coming," Pataki patted his jacket. Making his way out of the club he felt a chill that stopped him. He looked around into the many faces. Seeing nothing he shrugged it off.

Two hours had passed and both Unique and Infinite had moved from one section of the club to another where more attractive women could see them. Junior, seated five tables behind them watched their every move. Being a good looking man he recognized but pretended not to see the signs and signals the women were throwing his way. He was astonished by the way women made advances toward him nowadays and it was with this concept in mind that he had gotten the germ of an idea. He had already put the first part of his plan in motion when he reserved a hotel room next door to the club yesterday. He had returned last night through the back entrance, placing a female mannequin in the room's bed.

Unique and Infinite still at their table laughing about Unique's latest conquest. He had been telling Infinite about how the female demanded he handcuff and spank her before being allowed to sex her. And how he agreed to piss on her only when he did his urine accidently went up her now almost strangling her. Wiping tears from his eyes Unique nudged Infinite conspiratorially, and said, "Yo God, check that Shorty out right there, she's got that I wonna fuck you look and she's clocking you."

Infinite seen a very attractive brown skin woman in the company of her girlfriend smiling in his direction. He noticed how her finger kept touching her temple as if an attempt to hide her embarrassment. "Word God I see her, she shy, but I can tell she want it. But what about you? There's two of them God?"

"Naw, I'm still recuperating from that chick I just told you about. Besides, I promise Trisha I'd fuck her brains out when I get home tonight. But do your thing God. Call me in the morning and let me know how it was," Unique laughed.

Flagging down a waiter Infinite sent the women drinks on him.

Junior, sitting at a table behind the women heard the one holding her temple tell the other, "Girl this headache is kicking my ass and this loud ass music ain't making it no better." Before her girlfriend could reply the waiter appeared serving them drinks. When Infinite smiled at them, the one with the headache was about to send them back until her friend stopped her. "Girl don't be stupid, if that nigga thinks a drink is gonna get him some pussy tonight, let him, we're outta here in a little while anyway. Tell him thanks," they told the waiter. Catching the same waiter in transit Junior, acting as if he was gay, gave the waiter an envelope and a twenty dollar tip for making it seem like the envelope he delivered to Infinite came from the women.

"Damn God, you getting love letters from her already and shit. Open it and see what it say." Both men recognized the fragrance of Jasmine perfuming coming off the envelope. Smiling, infinite ripped it open and unfold the letter, a hotel room key fell out and into his lap. "What the fuck is . . ." Picking up the key he read the letter out loud: 'for the last hour I've been watching you—watching me. I hope you don't get the wrong idea about me for being so forward but I'm the kind of girl who don't believe in wasting time that could be better spent doing better things. Especially when it comes to getting the things I want, so when you've had your fill down here—come upstairs, I'm in room 112. And then the real fun can begin, Signed: Anticipation.'

"I told you! I told you!" Unique said shoving and slapping Infinite on the back.

Having finished their drinks and not wanting to give the two clowns at their table enough time to come to theirs, the women got up and made their way out of the club. Stopping at the men table the woman with the headache said to Infinite, "Thank you for the drinks that was awfully nice of you."

"It's a small token of my appreciation. Consider it my special way of showing that I think everything about you is nice."

Chuckling, she smiled and said, "See you later." The women pushed their way out of the club.

A half our later Unique told Infinite, "You better stop playing and go get that."

"Naw, not yet, not yet. Chill God I got this, I'ma let her sweat just a little bit. Let them panties get soak and wet.

Several minutes later Junior made his way out of the club and into the hotel room where he placed another envelope on the table near the door. Throughout the room he unscrewed all of the lamps light bulbs. Placing the mannequin in the bed and under the covers Junior went and hid in the room's closet leaving its door barely crack. He hadn't been waiting long before the room door open. Infinite tried the light switch when it didn't work, he seen Infinite squinting his eyes reading the card in the semi dark: 'I had a little headache so just wake me when you're ready.' A smile creased infinite's lips as he looked at the form in bed with the covers pulled over her head. "Shy huh," he mused as he stripped off his clothes heading for the shower. Less than two minutes into his shower the shower curtain was yanked to one side, and the last thing Infinite seen was a pillow before he heard the muffled explosion.

CHAPTER TWENTY-TWO

Junior sat in the back of his van holding one headphone to his ear eavesdropping on the conversation between unique and the crooked cop Pataki. The van was parked down the street from Unique's house. The music from crickets dominated the atmosphere in this suburban neighborhood.

It was close to Three o'clock in the morning, and before arriving here Junior had taken a can of nectar juice that was three by five inches long in size, and made a bomb out of it. He had first peeled the plastic lid from the can and drank the juice, and then poured a heavy concentration of gun powder from fireworks, ash-cans and m-80's into the small can, mixing it with a substance called Carbide Potassium Nitrate, until the can was filled. Taking a string coated in candle wax that was about four inches long, he placed one end of it into the can and let hot candle wax drip inside to hold it in place as the other end of the string hung outside of it like a fuse stem. The bomb was now in his pocket and ready to go.

On a small table next to him within the van laid a closed bottle of soda, only the soda had been replaced with gasoline. Next to this laid a small can of foam and a big industrial compartment inside his tight fitting vest pockets, and dropped his headphones to the seat. For now, he had heard all that he needed to hear from the conversation between the men. He knew that the men. He knew that the private security of this community drove around in a minivan and made their rounds every hour and a half and had left no more than five minutes ago. Careful to not disturb the quiet of

168

the night he bit down on his lower lip as he opened the van's door, quietly sliding it back just far enough for him to get out.

Hopping out of the van, the first thing he noticed was that it was a pale full moon.

When he was several cars away from the Lexus parked at the curb, as if he was now in a battle zone on enemy grounds, he dropped to the asphalt on the ground, and lying on his stomach, began to crawl towards the car he sought. He knew from prior investigation that the car had a viper alarm system which activated a voice warning before engaging its alarm. He also knew the alarm's radar detector would trigger if it caught him in its beams, he therefore decided to crawl below it so its radar detectors wouldn't detect him.

Reaching the front of the car now he turned on his back and pushed himself underneath it. Pulling the can of foam from his pocket he sprayed the alarm speaker with the shaving cream. This done, he scrambled back from beneath the car and quickly pop the hold. Using a screwdriver he removed his battery cable silenced the alarm the rung in a muffle. Using skillful hands he removed the top of the carburetor, this done, he turned the nectar can bomb upside down and placed it in to the intake manifold. Replacing the carburetor's cover he ran around the car to the driver's side and quickly jimmied the door climbing inside he began to pour gasoline on the floor. Making a quick exit, he returned to the front of the car and reconnected the battery cable, only this time the alarm made no muffled sounds, he knew this was because it was in the process of reprogramming itself to re-engage, which would take place within thirty seconds, but he was already four cars away by the time this happened.

Trisha's luscious and exposed ivory, drumstick of a thigh lay sprawled across Unique's dark body in bed. Neither of them was asleep. In fact they had just finished making love and now shared that moment of silence while marinating in love's aftermath.

Their love making was exceptional tonight, Trisha thought, different from all the other times, better, in fact, the best ever. This caused her now to indulge in the game call 'self-lie'. Meaning, she knew what lay at the heart of their love making being exceptionally good tonight but she was denying it, telling herself she should not have had such thoughts to begin with. Tonight was the first time she had ever fantasized about another man while having sex with Unique, up until now she thought it couldn't be done. It was a total stranger, the stranger she had let into her house over six weeks ago to check the smoke detectors.

Teddy, that was his name, Teddy the fire inspector. She had seen him only that once but he had put a fire inside of her that continued to flame on. She remembered vividly what he looked like as if his image had and presence had been branded on the memory script of her brain. He was tall, so dark and so very handsome. Muscles rippled through the shirt of his uniform and his pants had fitted snugly tight around his muscle-bound ass just the way she liked to see pants fitting a man.

From the moment he had entered her house she felt a powerful force of energy coming off of him. She thought he looked good wearing his cap, he had the right head, shape and face for it. Strong. Oval, chiseled African features. There wasn't a blemish nor one hair bump on his face—it made her want to reach out and touch it. The white of his eyes were so very clear, she knew it had a lot to do with good, clean living. They weren't bloodshot and they caressed her when she looked up into them. Trisha was snatched out of these reveries by the jolting ringing of the telephone. They both were accustom to getting calls this late and she knew that if it wasn't for Unique it was for her from her girlfriend down the block. They both had gotten in the habit of calling each other late at night to gossip as a means to keep each other company since both of their husbands kept late hours. In fact both women along with Jahborn's girlfriend, Monica had made plans to go out tomorrow night as girl's night out.

Reaching over Unique Trisha picked up the phone. "Hello . . . aye, what's up girlfriend . . . ? No, just laying here thinking, that's all. Huh? . . . the news?" She frowned, "Yeah, he's here hold on."

"Hello Unique, its be Barbara, Trisha's girlfriend from down the block and I was just telling her there's somebody on the news now with y'all last name."

Snatching the remote from the night table CNN news appeared on the screen recapping the most current event: 'Last night the bodies of yet two more men were found dead who had all the markings of the vigilante killer/slash Ghetto Soldier. The first man was identified as Larry Townsend of east new york Brooklyn, was found just outside of his home with a hole in his chest authorities say had been made from a bow and arrow. To date this appears to be the second killing of this kind within the last four months, authority further believe that these killings are all related." The anchorman droned on but by this time Unique had turned him out. "Another man was found shot to death inside a Manhattan hotel room."

Unique snapped off the covers as he sat up straight in bed. He almost was aware of Trisha mumbling something to her girlfriend on the phone as he flipped from channel to channel trying to catch the story again on the news as if to say hearing it for the second time would convince him that he was not dreaming. That his little brother Jahborn wasn't dead. Trisha hung up the phone and hugged him to her. His hands were balled into a fist as tears fell from his eyes. "I'm alright . . . I'm alright," he said pulling away from her, reaching for the phone.

"It's that vigilante guy isn't it Unique?"

Unique nodded his head, "But I don't know why Monica didn't call to tell us nothing, we gotta consider the fact that she might be dead too."

"He kills women too?"

Instead of responding to Trisha he barked into the phone, "Hello."

"Nigga, do you realize what time it is?"

"I don't give a fuck what time it is cause I'm sitting here watching the fucking news where I hear that my crew and now my little brother and his right hand man are dead. And I'm just wondering," Unique began to cry out loud, "Just what the fuck you intend to do about it cracker? The last time we met you assured me you would get this guy off my back, but you haven't delivered and as a result of it now two more of us are dead."

"Hold on."

Unique could hear the T.V. being turned on, on the other end of the phone to a news channel. "You still there?'

"Yeah I'm right fucking here," Unique seethed.

"Hey man, whadda you want from me—Christ, if I had the chance the guy would be on ice already, you know and I d—"

"Kill that shit Pataki. I don't pay you for excuses cracker, I pay you for results. What the fuck am I paying you for?"

"Listen to me you fucking monkey nigga, don't fucking tell me what my fucking job is, and you're paying me 'cause use know what's good for you. And if you keep running off at the mouth I'll come over there right now and kick your fucking head in you fucking egg plant."

"You know what Pataki, I'm beginning to think that you're scare to run into this guy, maybe you fear he'll take a big chunk outta your white ass. You know what else I been thinking—I been thinking if you really truly wanted to face off with this guy you would had put a tail on me and my guys since its obvious he's picking us off, but you didn't do that. Now for all I know Pataki, you and this motherfucker may be down together, side by side. Therefore, you know what else Pataki, I don't think I'll be needing your services anymore."

"Listen hear you n—," Pataki said until he heard the ringtone in his ear.

Unique hastily got dressed.

"Where you going Unique?" Trisha asked with both concern and fear in her voice.

"I gotta go to Brooklyn, gotta see for myself if my brother's at the morgue."

"I'm coming with you," she said heading for the clothes closet.

"No. Stay here and answer the phone in case Monica calls or someone else does. In fact call Monica I wonna know why that bitch ain't call us."

"I'm on it."

Outside, Unique pushed the button to disengage the car alarm. In his haste he hadn't paid attention to the fact that it made no sound but its doors unlocked. It was only after turning the keys in the ignition did he become aware of the powerful smell of the gasoline coming from within the car.

Trisha heard the loud explosions which had rattled the windows inside the house as well as the houses nearby. Not wanting to think the worse or that it could remotely involve Unique, and yet she couldn't stop herself from running out of the door to be sure. From where she stood now in total disbelief her eyes took in the sight of what was left of Unique's Lexus, with him inside, parts of him could be seen, wrapped in a ball of fire, trying to get out but the doors were jammed. Everyone could still hear him screaming from within. With very little clothes on Trisha rushed down the walkway crying and screaming for help. But no one could get near the car which by now had become a burning infernal. Her girlfriend Barbara and neighboring neighbors held on to her partly nude body to keep her from committing suicide.

CHAPTER TWENTY-THREE

Ignat's worse nightmare had come true. Her plan to get caught with Pataki by his wife had backfired because when his wife kicked him out he moved in with her, and was crueler now than before. He burnt her with cigarettes, kicked her to the floor and urinated on her. The only two items he had brought with him from home were his clock radio and his lamps from Tiffany.

Ignat's one bedroom apartment had been home for the last five years but with Pataki there now it became a prison.

Entering Ignat's small home from its door lead straight into a medium size living room. To the right of the door was a shute which passed itself off as a kitchen. To the left of the door and a few feet away was the bathroom. Several yards from the bathroom lay four steps which lead to her bedroom that she use to share with her daughter. Because this apartment was already small it became even smaller when Pataki, imposing himself, had moved in. Lately, he had been moving his clothes in a little at a time, which only served to clutter up his place. She had sent her daughter to stay at her mother's house for a while. She didn't trust him to be alone around her daughter. She knew he was a racist and was just using her, and as far as he knew, everybody else he came in contact with. He controlled her life and she hated the bastard. On the second day of moving in with her he had made a rule that whenever he came in, no matter what the hour, she had better be butt ass naked.

At the moment Ignat was in the refrigerator in the kitchen when she heard sounds of footsteps coming up the stairs in the hallway. Instinctively, she knew it was Pataki. Placing the three liter Pepsi back on the rack she ran into her room and stripped off all her clothes and was standing by her queen size bed when Pataki entered the room. He immediately began to loosen his tie and take off his clothes. Now totally nude himself, his eyes shifted down to her clothes on the floor.

He grinned and then looked back up into her face, "My nigga bitch been keeping her kitty cat covered while I've been gone, huh?" Closing the distance between them he leaned down to kiss her as he roughly forced two fingers inside of her cavity. Ignat's teeth clamp shut, she willed her thighs to do the same, but it was only her mind—her breath caught. Pataki breath stunk and he smelled of liquor. His face was flush, she knew he was drunk, she also knew that liquor and his temper equaled ass whipping.

He tried forcing his tongue inside her mouth but met clench teeth, and when she wouldn't budge he slapped her viciously across the face.

"Ahhhhh," Ignat weep stumbling sideways to the floor.

"What's the matter with you?" he huffed in mild irritation to which she knew could turn full force in a heartbeat. As she rose from the floor she knew if she didn't cooperate he would take pleasure by bringing her pain.

"My mouth still hurts from when you hit me last night, but I'm alright now, I'm alright. Can I get you something to drink or something to eat?"

"Now that's what I like to hear," he placed his gun in its holster on the night table before falling onto the bed, slapping sweat from his pock mark face. He wiggled his index finger, "Come here pussycat. After a long day of chasing after niggas, a man gets hungry," he grinned, "Did I tell you that your pussy tastes like fried chicken?" He giggled, wiping sweat from his face again. Ignat climbed carefully towards him on the bed, "Yeah, you told me," she said remembering he told her the reason her pussy taste like chicken was because she was a nigga and niggas loved to eat chicken. She knew what he wanted her to do now having done it many times before. And though she could not stand to be near him, it was the closest thing she could do to humiliate him, though to him she knew it was a turn on.

She stood above Pataki's head on the bed grabbing on to the railing to support her weight as she lowered herself down over his face in a squatting position and began to grind her gash roughly across his face. Pataki's stiff tongue worked itself in and out of her cavity as if it was a pencil sharpener. After a while of this she fought desperately, but was slowly losing the battle in fighting against the sensational pleasures that it was bringing her. Throwing her head back she grind even harder against him.

Several minutes later she was panting as light beads of perspiration glistened across her top lip and forehead. She felt the muscles in her inner thighs starting to tingle and tighten as the low, slow, but pleasurable feeling began to move towards the center of her being. Suddenly her insides began to erupt. She was buckling and plowing harder now and could feel him sucking the juice out of her as if it was the spirit of her soul. Suddenly she heard the degenerate bastard gagging as her flood gate opened and came pouring out. He pushed her off of him as he choked. Using the bed rails she stood up and looked down into Pataki's now greasy, sticky face. Looking further down her eyes caught sight of his poor excuse of a dick and how it too was bitching for conversation now. Before he could do anything further she jumped off the bed and rushed out of the room.

"Hey!" he yelled, "come back here. Where you're going?"

He could not see the evil grin on her face when she called back, "to the kitchen to get something to drink you want something?"

"Yeah, a Bacardi dark and hurry back bitch, I got something for ya!"

It was then that Ignat realized she was going to poison him.

Junior was on his knees in the hallway with his ear to the door listening for sounds before he picked the lock. Though he hadn't heard anything within the last few seconds, he knew Pataki was inside his black girlfriend's apartment. Without another moment to waste he went to work on the cylinder and the lock sprung. He duck-walked himself into the apartment now with gun in hand.

Just as he was about to close the door behind him he heard the faint sounds of footsteps and halted his actions. Before he had the chance to move, duck of hide somewhere the light skin woman popped into his vision. Startled, the smirk on her face dropped as she gave a light yelp and then covered her mouth as she realized the mistake of making a sound. Seeing the panic expression on her face caused Junior to spring into action before she could do anything stupid. He closed the distance between them in a flash with his gun pointed at her face, he covered her mouth. The woman made no attempt to cover her totally nude body. He faintly heard her muffled whisper through his fingers, "please mister, don't kill me, take what you want, whatever you want, but just don't hurt me." Junior could tell that someone had done one helluva job of that already as he noticed the web mark on the swollen left side of her face.

"I'm not here to hurt you and if you do as I say, I won't."

She nodded her head in understanding.

"Your lover—the white guy," he whispered, moving her further into the small living room, "He's here isn't he? Where is he?"

She didn't hesitate in answering when he removed his hand from her mouth, "the racist bastard's in the bedroom."

"Alright, here's what I want you to d-"

"Don't move you motherfucker," Junior heard the raspy voice behind him warn. Although he couldn't see who it was he knew it was Pataki, the horrifying look on the woman's face told him so. Pataki thought he had heard voices coming from the living room and knew that Ignat was not in the habit of talking to herself. At first he thought she was on the phone until he picked up the extension in the bedroom and heard the dial tone.

He knew he was not going crazy and felt compelled to investigate, taking his service revolver with him, and was now glad that he did. From the looks of the guy standing in the living room wearing all black and a ski mask, he fitted the description of the man who was most wanted by the authorities in all the five boroughs.

Pataki could not believe his great fortune—the guy was now standing in his living room—well Ignat's living room, which to him meant the same thing. But what he couldn't understand was why was the guy there, he wasn't a drug dealer, he was a cop, so what was the guy doing here. And then it dawned on him that he was probably here for Ignat, she knew the guy all the while and probably had been feeding him all the information he had been feeding her while in bed at night about the investigation they had lodged against this guy. Wow what a smuck I've been, he told himself, well I'm going to lock both of their asses up now, he decided.

Junior's back was still to Pataki and therefore knew he could not see the gun he held in his hand. Judging from Pataki's commanding voice Junior knew that Pataki was holding a gun as well.

Ignat attempted to move away from him but Pataki admonished her. "You too bitch, don't fucking move a muscle," he said thinking all the while that perhaps he should first humiliate her by making her go down on him in front of her friend, before calling for back up to lock them up. Junior surmised by the sound of Pataki's voice that he was behind and to the left of him. He slowly moved his left arm away from his body. He did this for two reasons, the first was to get Pataki talking some more so he could get a precise placing of him and the second reason was so he could shoot him from an angle beneath his left armpit. He raised his arm another inch now and heard the ugly sound of the hammer on Pataki's gun being cocked back. "I'm going to get you closer to god real quick nigga if you try that again," Pataki said making his way slowly down the house steps. Seeing the frighten look in the woman's eyes told Junior she was more afraid of the cop than he was. The creaking sounds Pataki made on the steps told Junior he was getting closer and knew he had to make his move.

He raised his arm just a little more to assure he got a clean shot, only this time he was punished for his actions. True to his word Pataki squeezed the trigger; the woman began to scream when she heard the loud roar. The first bullet hit Junior in the upper back, two more hit him in the lower region, but his body armor took the impact. Realizing that this was it, now or never, stumbling forward, just as he turned around to get a better aim, he was shot in the face. Falling back even further now he was still trying to face his man, raising his gun hand, but he heard the roar and felt the impact of another bullet as it hit him in the forearm with a force that made his gun hand fly out of control and the gun dropped from his hand. He fell to the floor a few feet away from it. Breathing labored from having the air knocked out of him, he lay on his back on the floor staring up at the ceiling watching it spin.

He thought about how ironic it was that the crooked cop would be the one who took him out. The hunter finally got captured by the game. He could still hear the woman screaming until he heard her being hit and told, "Shut the fuck up you nigga bitch." He couldn't see the woman nor Pataki but their voices told him they were close. Suddenly Pataki's face hovered on top of him, he could see the gun he held in his hand. The cop's face reminded him of a rat. From far away he heard the cop speak, "I knew it, I knew it was a nigga. There's no black cream smeared on your face underneath that mask, but you're about to be a dead nigga now."

Junior seen Pataki raising his gun leveling it with the center of his head, his finger was inside the trigger guard, tightening, slowly pulling the trigger until suddenly there was a loud explosion, and another one and another one. Junior realized he was dying, he had to be, Pataki had shot three more times and yet he hadn't felt a thing.

He became confused when he seen Pataki's eyes began to bugle, stretching wider and wider as the vein in his forehead strained against its skin. Pataki's legs moved now in baby-like steps as if they weighed a ton as he turned around to look behind him to learn what had happened, but it was suddenly too much of an effort. Before he could turn around completely he fell to the floor partially on top of Junior. Using his good hand he took the gun out of Pataki's hand when he realized he was still breathing. He pushed the cop off of him as best he could and then tried to sit himself up in a prone position, and there, standing in the doorway he seen a miniature version of himself dressed in ski mask and all black. He recognized the eyes which stared back at him from behind the mask and couldn't believe what he was seeing.

"Your Boo Bear is here, don't worry Daddy," Kim said now rushing to her father, kneeling down beside him. She saw blood oozing out of both sides of his face mask. Luckily for Junior the bullet had entered his left jaw and exits his right. But the shot in the forearm was serious; a nerve had been damaged, which could be told by the way his arm continued to jump on the floor.

Seeing all the blood, Kim knew she had to get her father out of there and fast or else he would bleed to death. She looked around her, not knowing what to do, or how she would lift him.

Ignat, the woman at this time would be no help, she was still in shock and had slid to the floor with her back against the wall, her legs were spread wide and she rocked back and forth.

Now that the room had stop spinning and everything came back into focus Junior grunted, "Help me up." Using his good hand he turned on his side and slowly climbed to his feet while Kim, on the other side of him strained to help keep his balance. Standing steady now, Junior seen Pataki's eyes open. Junior nodded his head toward his gun lying on the floor telling Kim to go get it. Rushing over she scooped it up, sticking it in her waist before returning underneath her father's armpit to support him.

People from the building were now beginning to crowd the doorway as Junior and his daughter headed towards it. Suddenly, Junior stopped, turned around and walked slowly back to where Pataki laid. Standing over him Junior cocked the hammer on the gun. Pataki tried to grin but failed, and then croaked in a strained raspy voice, "You . . . . can't . . . can't kill me . . . I'ma . . . I'ma cop . . . you'll," he gasped, licked his lips and said, "They'll fr-fry you . . . if you do!"

Junior wince as he leaned down closer to Pataki and said, "You're not a cop . . . you're a coward pretending to be a cop but you're really a racist pig. You've hid behind that badge long enough, and now your time has expired." Junior squeezed the trigger. Blood from Pataki's head slapped against the arm of Junior's black sweat suit, chest and face mask. Standing up straight again he almost lost his balance but Kim caught him and held him steady. Together both Junior and his daughter made their way out of the apartment. People in the doorway got out of their way, giving them more than enough room to get by.

*   *   *

As the 747 at Kennedy Airport ascended into the sky Junior Washington sat in the first class section with his arm in a sling again. Using his good hand, he held a cellular phone to his ear listening intently to the party on the other end of the line. "All of your reservations and arrangements in Tahiti have been made, but we're going to miss you here Junior!"

Smiling, Junior replied, "My family and I will miss all of you tremendously as well Senator Johnson, and from the basement of our hearts we thank you all, for everything!" The line was then disconnected.

As Junior fold the cellular phone close, Karla, sitting next to him, looked up from the bank accounts on the screen of the lab top sitting in her lap, having never seen so much money before, she shook her head and smiled. Returning her smile, Junior then looked across the aisle to the seat adjacent to his, where his daughter sat with a pair of Sony headphones on, reading an article in a 'Source' magazine. When she realized that both of her parents were looking at her, she turned their way and they all smiled.

THE END

OTHER BOOKS WRITTEN BY THE AUTHOR

Glock Boys

The Other Side Of The Crack Vial

Love Jones

Get Money